The rush of fe
Mac the mom
made him wa
head and roa

Or just sweep her into his arms and never let her go. He was filled with elation, near to trembling with it, and that shocked him more than anything else.

He could not—would not—let Sabrina affect him like this. Emotion was danger. Emotion hurt. He'd learned that all too easily when his mother died. And caring about someone too much, especially a woman, could destroy a man. Hadn't his own father nearly suffered that fate?

No, he had to be strong and self-contained. He would be a good husband to Sabrina. He would treat her kindly, keep her in the style to which she was already well accustomed, but he would not let her get too close.

Dear Reader,

I always think January's a long and dreary month—particularly if I'm broke thanks to the sales! If you're like me and want to spice up your life, then you've come to just the right place. I'd be hard-pushed to name a favourite out of the four books on offer this month; they're all *Sensational!*

Let's start with the lady you might not have met before, **Sharon Sala**; I can guarantee that you'll see more of her and that you'll really love the dark and dangerous Justice brothers. This month *Ryder's Wife* is the title to look for and in March keep your eyes peeled for *Roman's Heart*. I'm betting that this talented author is going to be an established favourite in no time.

Next up, comes a strong and sexy tale from **Maura Seger**—*Possession*. Mac Donnelly thought he was going to teach Sabrina Giacanna a lesson, but that's not the way it worked out...

Continuing her THE PROTECTORS mini-series **Beverly Barton** gives us *Guarding Jeannie*, and **Maggie Shayne** revisits her popular Brand family in *The Husband She Couldn't Remember*. Ben Brand's beloved wife suddenly turns up out of the blue—but he thought she was dead!

It's all happening in Silhouette Sensation®. Come back and visit again, won't you?

The Editor

Possession

MAURA SEGER

DID YOU PURCHASE THIS BOOK WITHOUT A COVER?

If you did, you should be aware it is **stolen property** as it was reported *unsold and destroyed* by a retailer. Neither the author nor the publisher has received any payment for this book.

All the characters in this book have no existence outside the imagination of the author, and have no relation whatsoever to anyone bearing the same name or names. They are not even distantly inspired by any individual known or unknown to the author, and all the incidents are pure invention.

All Rights Reserved including the right of reproduction in whole or in part in any form. This edition is published by arrangement with Harlequin Enterprises II B.V. The text of this publication or any part thereof may not be reproduced or transmitted in any form or by any means, electronic or mechanical, including photocopying, recording, storage in an information retrieval system, or otherwise, without the written permission of the publisher.

This book is sold subject to the condition that it shall not, by way of trade or otherwise, be lent, resold, hired out or otherwise circulated without the prior consent of the publisher in any form of binding or cover other than that in which it is published and without a similar condition including this condition being imposed on the subsequent purchaser.

Silhouette, Silhouette Sensation and Colophon are registered trademarks of Harlequin Books S.A., used under licence.

*First published in Great Britain 1999
Silhouette Books, Eton House, 18-24 Paradise Road,
Richmond, Surrey TW9 1SR*

© Seger Inc. 1998

ISBN 0 373 07843 9

18-9901

*Printed and bound in Spain
by Litografia Rosés S.A., Barcelona*

MAURA SEGER

and her husband, Michael, married after a whirlwind
courtship that might have been taken directly from a
romance. To date, she has written more than ten books for
Silhouette®. She finds that writing each book is an
adventure filled with fascinating people who never fail to
surprise her. When she isn't writing, Maura keeps busy
homeschooling her two children and thinking of new
stories.

Other novels by Maura Seger

Silhouette Sensation®

Legacy
Sea Gate
Day and Night
Sir Flynn and Lady Constance
Man Without a Memory
Heaven in His Arms

Silhouette Desire®

Cajun Summer
Treasure Hunt
Princess McGee

Silhouette Special Edition®

A Gift Beyond Price

Silhouette Christmas Stories 1988
'Starbright'

Chapter 1

Where the hell was the mixer crew?

Mac Donnelly climbed out of the excavation that took up most of a city block and glanced around quickly. The mixer was running, all right, but there was no sign of the men who should have been standing by, ready to start pouring the footings. Hands on his lean hips, he scowled. It wasn't as though there weren't enough problems already with this job.

He'd been suspicious of the soil reports from the beginning, and now he was damn glad he'd insisted on having them redone even with the delay it caused. Putting a fifty-story building on top of fill wasn't his idea of a walk in the park, but it would be a hell of a lot worse if he didn't know exactly what he was up against. He'd gotten the footings redesigned, he was ready to go, now all he needed were the men.

The men who were currently at the far end of the construction site where it butted up against a row of nineteenth-century brownstones.

Mac could see the workers through the gate in the fence. They were standing bunched together, grins painted on their mugs, downing glasses of...what was that stuff? *Lemonade?*

''Who decided it was break time?'' The cold lash of his voice broke the cozy little group apart. The men looked startled by his sudden appearance, then worried. Mac took due note of their reaction and approved of it. He was a fair boss, he never asked a worker to do anything he wouldn't do himself and he treated people with respect. But he called the shots and he expected to be obeyed. A construction site wasn't a democracy. He was in charge and every man there knew it.

They also knew they weren't supposed to be standing around, drinking lemonade and looking like a bunch of fools.

''Last time I checked,'' Mac said, ''we had footings to pour.'' He was about to add something else when the thought went clean out of his head. The men had stepped aside enough to reveal a woman standing in their midst, holding a tray and watching him with eyes so wide they reminded him instantly of a startled kitten.

''Who the hell are you?'' he demanded. The kitten impression got stronger by the moment. She was petite, possibly as much as a foot shorter than him, and she looked...soft. Very, very soft. From the short blond curls that hugged her head to the surprisingly long legs beneath the white apron tied snugly around her curvy hips, the impression she gave was overwhelmingly feminine in a way that was not remotely politically correct.

Even he, with all his healthy cynicism, felt a sudden, almost irresistible urge to gather her up in his arms and protect her from any harm the world might attempt. The sensation astounded him and put all his defenses on high alert. That it came right along with other urges of a very *different* nature didn't help.

"Who am *I?*" the kitten said. She put down the tray on a nearby barrel, folded her arms across her chest and glared at him. "Who are *you?*"

Mac did a long, slow double take. A kitten with claws. Better and better. The smile he gave her was flat out predatory.

The other men weren't smiling. They were closing in around the little blonde again with the clear intent of doing exactly what Mac felt he—and he alone—ought to be doing. Protecting her.

"She didn't know, boss. She—"

"—just being nice—"

"—moved some boxes for her—"

"—didn't take long—"

"—hot and all—"

"—no harm, just—"

"—helping out for a minute—"

Mac scowled. He stared again at the center of all the turmoil, the reason work on his site had ground to a halt. She didn't so much as flinch, but matched him glare for glare. Her right foot began to tap.

"Back to work," he ordered.

The men hesitated, but only for an instant. With apologetic looks at the blonde, they set their glasses on the tray and vamoosed.

Sabrina watched them go with carefully concealed alarm. The man who remained—the one standing directly in front of her—was very…very…*everything*. He was bare-chested, which shouldn't have mattered. She'd seen plenty of bare chests—who hadn't?—but none as perfectly, massively muscled. Plus, she was getting an impression—a sense really—of a will that matched those incredible male contours all too well. The man had her just plain *rambling*.

She never rambled. She was calm, clear-headed and reasonable. Just who was this guy to have this effect on her?

"I'm Mac Donnelly," he said and held out his hand. He was watching her very carefully, his eyes narrowed, as though gauging her response.

His hand was calloused, the skin on the palm only slightly lighter than the burnished skin pulled taut over long bones and hard muscle. He had black hair worn longish, curling at the nape of his neck. Black hair also curled in a line down his chest, disappearing beneath the waistband of jeans that hugged his narrow hips. His eyes, when she remembered to look at them, were a startling blue.

Deceit of any kind did not come easily to Sabrina. According to her father, that reason alone made her unfit for any role in the family business. However, she was learning to fudge a little when she really thought she had to. "Sabrina…Giacanna," she said and felt her hand swallowed by his. "I'm sorry if I caused a problem."

He shrugged those massive shoulders. "You didn't. The men know what I expect." His voice had gentled. It sent a shiver clear through her.

He let go of her then, but only after giving her the distinct impression that he would have preferred not to. With a glance at the building behind her, he asked, "You work there?"

"I'm helping out a friend. It's her restaurant—she's the chef—but her little girl is sick, so I'm filling in."

"Are you married?"

No beating around the bush for Mac Donnelly. His forthrightness shocked her, coming as she did from an environment where few ever said what they meant and usually only then by accident. Not that she was about to let him see her surprise. "No, I'm not. Are you?"

"No. Now that we've covered that, how about having dinner with me tonight?"

Sabrina stared at him. She was used to men who were a whole lot less direct and a whole lot more cautious. Men who looked at her bottom line instead of her bottom. But then, it was just smart to be that way when dealing with Rourk Talveston's little girl. Except Mac Donnelly didn't know that. *He didn't know.*

"I have to work…." She shouldn't have let her refusal just trail off. She should have said something decisive, but decisiveness was sometimes a problem for her. Not all the time, though, not with the really important stuff.

Was Mac Donnelly really important stuff?

"All night?" he asked and that smile was back. His eyes had a little gray in them, a wolf's gray. Funny how she hadn't noticed that sooner.

"No, not all night—"

"I'll come by when you close. What does a chef like to eat when she isn't cooking?"

She could get lost in those eyes if she wasn't careful. "Leftovers. I hate throwing anything out, especially when I'm just subbing." Absolutely the only way she was willing to deal with Mac Donnelly was on her own territory.

She could see him weighing her suggestion and knew the exact moment he decided to give the advantage to her, for now.

"Sounds good. What time?"

She told him. He nodded, gave her another of those long, slow looks and went back to work. Just once, he glanced over his shoulder and caught her watching. She got another grin for that.

Once she was back in the relative coolness of the kitchen—the ovens weren't going full blast yet—Sabrina leaned against a counter and took a deep breath. She couldn't believe she'd agreed to see Mac Donnelly just like that. Where was her natural caution, her good sense, her normal reserve? Granted, she was going through an upheaval in her life, and had made some tough choices lately. But that didn't excuse agreeing to a date with a stranger on the basis of a few minutes of conversation.

Thank heaven she'd at least kept her wits about her enough to insist they meet at the restaurant. She would be able to call the shots, set the tone, stay in control. She would be okay. Never mind that she hadn't dated in over a year and hadn't been very good at it back then. Never mind that her heart was hammering against her ribs and had been since her first glance at Mac Donnelly.

Who was he anyway? A foreman, most likely, but young for a job the size of the one next door. Maybe he was a crew chief. Whatever he was, he worked with his hands—grunt work, her father would have called it. She hadn't Rourk Talveston's disdain for manual labor, but then, unlike him, she'd never done it.

A smile lifted the corners of her full mouth. In another few hours, it would be ninety degrees plus in the kitchen. She would have half a dozen orders going simultaneously while she also kept an eye on all the *sous chefs*. She would be on her feet and in nonstop motion. Before the night was over, she could easily sweat off a pound or two. But that wasn't manual labor, that was haute cuisine.

She laughed, tucked Mac Donnelly away in the back of her mind and turned her attention to the pepper and crab bisque.

She didn't know. He'd been watching, and he was willing to swear that his name had meant absolutely nothing to her. For the first time in a whole lot longer than he cared to remember, he'd met a woman he wanted who had no reason to see him as anything other than a man.

And what a woman. She looked the way she did, she cooked *and* she had actually blushed when he asked if she was married. With her blond hair and incredible violet eyes, Sabrina Giacanna got to him in ways he wouldn't have thought possible. Not that he was vulnerable, absolutely not. He was just out for a little R and R. If that was what she wanted, great. If not, that was fine, too.

No sweat. Well, none except for the rivulets that poured down his back and chest over the next couple of hours as he worked with the men to get the first footings laid. In the almost spongy fill, the footings had to be extended so far that they merged into each other, forming a foundation mat for the steel columns that would rise above. He'd insisted the mat be run all the way to bedrock and made hollow so that it basically floated. It was an expensive, time-consuming technique, but it was also the best way to go. And Mac Donnelly liked the best. In business, in women, in life. But unlike the buildings he put up, he wasn't inclined to do any settling.

Ten hours later, he glanced up from the paperwork he forced himself to complete at the end of each day. The construction site was quiet. Except for the trailer he used as an office and the watchmen already on duty, the place was empty. Not so next door. The ground floor of the brownstone was lit up. Every once in a while, he could see a shadow move across the windows where he supposed the kitchen must be. Nobody popped out the back, no waiter sneaking a smoke, no busboy taking a break. Sabrina Giacanna might be a substitute, but it looked as though she ran a tight ship. Or maybe it was just that everyone felt that same weird need to protect that had hit him so hard the first moment he looked at her.

He stood and stretched the kinks out of his back and shoulders. By now he ought to be used to the hours he had to put in behind a desk, but he still resented them. It had been a lot simpler back in the days when his father and uncle were running things. Before it all went so wrong.

The security guards waved to him as he drove off. One of them carefully closed and locked the gate behind the pearl-gray sports car. Traffic was tough as usual but Mac scarcely noticed. Maneuvering into the garage under his building, he pulled to a stop, got out and flipped the key to the attendant.

"I'll be going out again, but I'm taking the pickup. Pull it round the front for me, will you?"

"Sure thing, Mr. Donnelly."

In the elevator, Mac punched in his security code and waited. Moments later, the doors slid open directly onto his apartment. Ignoring the panoramic view of Manhattan that the floor-to-ceiling windows provided, he strode toward his bedroom suite. Less than forty-five minutes later, showered, shaved and dressed, he was back downstairs.

* * *

Sabrina exhaled for what felt like the first time in hours. The last of the paying customers were finishing their demitasses, much of the staff had already left for the night and she actually had a few minutes to get ready for her pseudo-date.

That was how she'd decided to think of it. It wasn't a real date. They weren't going out. She was cooking for him, which was her job, after all, so there would be that nice, safe veneer of professionalism between them. Much better than a *date* date.

All the same, she didn't particularly want to look like the drowned rabbit she felt. A quick dash into the ladies' room confirmed her worst fears. With a groan, she grabbed for her bag, fished around and managed to find an actual lipstick and some blush. It helped, but not a lot. There was never anything she could do with her hair. It was just too baby fine and curled too much, so she left it alone. But that apron—

Oh, my God, the apron. She looked as though she'd crawled through dinner, not cooked it. With another, more frantic glance at the clock, she ripped off the offending garment and quickly donned another. A fresh toque might be a good idea, too. If nothing else, the traditional white chef's hat made her look taller. On second thought, she decided the accessory was too much. She was back in the kitchen, pretending to go over the specials for the following evening when her cousin, Joseph, the maître d', stuck his head in.

"Your guest is here, Sabrina." The frown that accompanied his announcement spoke volumes. Joseph was just barely thirty, a compact, muscular man, who was very married to his grade-school sweetheart and blessed with five sisters, seven nieces and two beautiful little daughters. He adored them all but had a far chillier attitude toward his fellow males, most of whom he thought sadly lacking in proper appreciation for what was surely God's greatest gift to man— women. Sabrina took one quick look in his direction and guessed Mac was not going to get the Joseph seal of approval.

With confidence she was far from feeling, she said, "Thank you. I think we're all done. I'll lock up."

"It's no trouble for me to stay."

"I appreciate that, but it isn't necessary. Besides," she added with a smile, "Sylvia would never forgive me for making you get home late."

"She would understand," Joseph insisted gravely. For good measure, he glanced toward the outer room, then added, "When I explain the circumstances."

"No, don't do that," Sabrina said hastily. She could just imagine where any such explanation would lead and she absolutely was not up to dealing with it.

"We're just going to talk about business," she said in a rare burst of deceit.

Joseph's eyebrows rose eloquently. "Business?"

"He works on the construction site next door."

Remarkably—indeed, miraculously—a ray of light appeared in his dark Sicilian stare. "Ahh, he knows your father."

It wasn't exactly a question and the shrug Sabrina offered in response wasn't exactly an answer. It was possible Mac Donnelly knew *of* her father. Plenty of people did.

Having convinced himself that Sabrina's companion for the evening would have the sense to behave himself, Joseph left. Sabrina sighed with relief that was short-lived. Remembering her manners, she hurried into the dining room.

"I'm sorry," she said with a smile. "There were just a few things I needed to—"

Finish up. That was what she'd meant to say and would have if she'd remembered, but she didn't because just then her heart slammed up against her ribs and her stomach did a loooong, sloooow dive. It was all she could do to remember to breathe.

There was something fundamentally unfair about a man looking as good as Mac did in a cotton shirt, khakis and a blue blazer. She could excuse her reaction to him when he was stripped to the waist with all his astonishing muscles on display, but surely she ought to have better control of herself now.

"Hi," she said. With further shock, she realized he was returning the intentness of her gaze, and then some. There was nothing rude or blatant in his regard, but she was left with the undeniable impression that Mac Donnelly didn't miss very much.

"Hi," he said and smiled.

Some moments later, Sabrina realized she was hearing the ticking of the grandfather clock that graced the entrance to the restaurant. It reverberated in the silence neither one of them had thought to break, so absorbed were they in each other.

Suddenly self-conscious, she resisted the nervous instinct to touch her hair, a habit broken in cooking school, and gestured toward the back.

"There's a special table in the kitchen kept for guests who are friends of the owners. Would that be all right with you?"

He nodded but said nothing, still seemingly content to look at her. She was vividly aware of his gaze as she led the way to the kitchen. The dining room they passed through was elegant in the extreme, the walls paneled in the original burled walnut dating from the building's construction over a hundred years before, the tables covered with handmade lace tablecloths and spaced at discreet intervals to allow for private conversation. It occurred to Sabrina that Mac might not be too comfortable in such surroundings. She was glad to have the alternative of the kitchen.

He paused just inside the big double doors and looked around with genuine interest. The kitchen wasn't huge by restaurant standards, running thirty feet in one direction and about fifteen in the other. Into that space was crammed a walk-in refrigerator and freezer, three six-burner gas stoves with ovens, a separate wall convection oven and a central counter that held the main preparation areas and also served as storage. Above it stretched a steel frame adorned with hooks that held pots, pans and skillets of virtually every description.

The frenzy of dinner preparations had ended long before, which had allowed the temperature to cool to a more tolerable level. Even so, it was undeniably warm in the kitchen. A light breeze entered through the windows that stood wide open to the evening air.

"How many dinners did you serve?" Mac asked as he continued glancing around.

"Fifty-seven," Sabrina replied automatically although the question surprised her. People generally asked about the various pieces of equipment or the restaurant's specialties. The business end didn't seem to occur to very many.

"Is that about typical for a weeknight?"

"So I understand. The restaurant has been here for five years, and it was successful from the beginning."

They were talking business. Not the construction business, to be sure, but business all the same. After her claim to quiet Joseph, there was a certain justice to it.

"Do you have an interest in the hospitality industry?" she asked.

"The what? Oh, no, not particularly." Some of the buildings he'd put up had restaurants on their ground floors, and some of those were very well known. Since his usual deal called for him to keep part ownership after construction was completed, he saw a portion of his income from the restaurant rentals, but they were just one small part of a much larger picture. Not that he was about to go into any of that with the lovely Sabrina Giacanna.

And she was lovely, all right, with her cheeks becomingly flushed and her hair in disarray. He noticed that she wasn't wearing the usual chef's getup, just a simple apron that hugged her curves very nicely—very distractingly. He found himself watching her hands as she began laying out various implements. She wore no polish and her nails were clipped short. Her fingers were long and slender, the bones delicately formed. A thin white scar ran along her left thumb from the knuckle to the base.

Without thinking, he reached out and lightly traced a finger along the scar. ''What happened?''

She jerked slightly in surprise. ''My first term at cooking school, I thought I knew how to handle a knife.'' Her laugh was breathy. ''Turned out I was wrong.''

He nodded and stepped back a pace, giving them both a little room. Just then, he needed the space and that surprised him. He'd wanted her from the first, he was honest enough to admit, but the hot, driving need he felt stunned him. The only bigger surprise was the strange pang of regret he experienced at the mere thought of her being hurt. That protective feeling again. He could see how that instinct could get to be a real nuisance real quick.

''What's for dinner?'' he asked.

An hour later, Mac leaned back in his chair, surveyed the woman across from him and grinned. ''Okay, I'm convinced, you can cook.''

Sabrina gave him a startled look. ''Did you think I was pulling a fast one?'' She sounded a little nervous again, which surprised him since she'd settled down nicely over the course of the meal. He'd deliberately kept the conversation light, steering it away from anything too personal that might reveal more about himself than he was willing to.

She had a sense of humor and a breathtaking smile to go with it. And there was a certain shyness about her he found intriguing. She had no hard edges and few defenses, he sensed, compared to the women he had known. He couldn't help wondering how that could be.

It was on the tip of his tongue to say that he didn't think she would know how to pull a fast one, but he caught himself. As absurd as it sounded, the comment might hurt her feelings and he didn't want to do that.

He told himself it was because any woman who could produce the kind of meal she had deserved the utmost courtesy, but he knew there was a hell of a lot more to it than that.

Still, dinner had been spectacular. He'd never paid much attention to food, but if he was going to be spending time with Sabrina Giacanna—and he had made up his mind that he was—he just might start.

"What's this dessert again?" he asked.

"Pears glazed in brandy and baked in 'thousand leaves' pastry topped with crème fraîche."

"It's not bad." When she raised an eyebrow, he relented. "It's incredible. The whole meal was incredible. But I can't always expect you to cook, chef or not. So I'm sitting here wondering where it'll be safe to take you when we go out."

The other eyebrow went up. *"When?"*

He refilled their glasses with the slightly sweet white Bordeaux that accompanied dessert. "Now you see, that's the kind of situation where men and women run into trouble.''

She'd run out of raised eyebrows but her skepticism still made itself felt.

"Suppose I'd said *if* we go out? How would you have felt?''

Sabrina hesitated. He was too clever. Clever enough to keep her from learning very much about him over dinner, and clever enough now to turn any objection she had right back on her.

"It's an 'on the one hand, other hand' kind of thing,'' she admitted. "I'd feel you weren't taking anything for granted, but I'd also wonder if you were actually interested.''

"I'm not and I am. Better now?''

She didn't answer but instead asked, "So what got you started pouring concrete?''

Her choice of words jarred him slightly although he didn't pause to ponder why, not just then. "Somebody's got to do it. Besides, it pays well.''

That seemed to make sense to her. She nodded. "Have you been with Century long?''

There it was again, that little jarring sensation. She hadn't said Century Construction, just Century, as though she'd heard of it before, actually knew of it. But why would she? Why would a drop-dead gorgeous woman who cooked like a dream and helped out a sick friend in her restaurant have any awareness at all of anything to do with construction?

"Ten years,'' he said. "Since it started up.'' He was watching her more carefully now, not just appreciating

the way the light played over her delicate features as
he had been doing up until then. His senses were on
high alert, as when he walked the high steel. He felt
the quiet deep inside, the stillness of the hunter, when
he allowed nothing to distract him from the job at
hand.

"You must really like the work."

He shrugged. "It beats being stuck behind a desk
all day." Since too much of his day was spent behind
a desk, he figured he knew what he was talking about.

"I feel that way about cooking. I can't imagine a
job where I'd have to sit still. It's funny, though—and
you must have noticed how people tend to look down
on jobs that require physical effort. Oh it's all right if
you're a 'star' in some way, an athlete or a really
famous chef, like that. But otherwise, people seem to
think that success means your own office and lots of
meetings to attend."

Mac grimaced. That would describe his own life all
too well if he let it. He was famous—or infamous—
for making the bankers and the security analysts, the
"suits" as he thought of them, come out to whatever
site he was on to talk to him while he did what he
described as "real" work. He'd drawn the line at holding meetings on the high steel although the idea still
tempted him from time to time.

"Was your family disappointed when you decided
to become a chef?" he asked.

Sabrina hesitated. Her father hadn't been disappointed. He hadn't been…anything, mainly because he
hadn't believed for a second that she meant it.

''My dad didn't take it seriously,'' she said, weighing her words.

''Your mom?''

''She died when I was a baby.''

''That's rough.'' No platitudes from Mac, not even any after-the-fact sympathy. Just truth.

''I suppose it is,'' she said quietly. ''But since I never had a mother, I don't really know what I missed.'' The words rang hollow even to herself. It was just something she'd come to terms with a long time ago. Or at least, she thought she had.

''My mother died when I was young, too,'' Mac said quietly. He looked at Sabrina for a long moment. Her eyes really were incredible. For the first time, he understood the ancient belief that they were the mirrors of the soul. ''I can't remember the last time I mentioned that to anyone.''

''I don't talk about it, either,'' Sabrina said. In the silence that drew out between them was the shared realization that they were both in uncharted territory.

''I'll help you clear up,'' Mac said finally. She nodded, relieved by the mundane chore. He made her think all too much, this man who by all rights should only make her feel. He was easily the most quintessentially male being she had ever encountered. Just looking at him sent her libido into overdrive. That primal reaction should have been enough. Her mind should have been safe from him, safe and in control. But it wasn't. Nothing was.

There was little enough tidying to do and it was accomplished quickly. The main overhead lights were

now off, leaving the kitchen in soft shadows. Faint
aromas of herbs and wine lingered on the air. Sabrina
wiped her hands dry, ignored the fluttering in her
stomach and summoned up a courteous smile. "I hope
you enjoyed dinner." She sounded very professional,
the caring chef.

Mac frowned slightly and took a step closer to her.
Instinctively she stepped back only to come up against
the counter. Her hands closed on the edge of it. Her
smile wobbled just a little but she got it back under
control quickly, or she thought she did.

"What are you afraid of?" Mac demanded. His
voice was low and slightly rough.

Her eyes widened. A lifetime's practice of concealing her emotions had left her ill prepared even to acknowledge them inwardly, much less have them per-
ceived with such blunt accuracy by a man who was a
virtual stranger.

"I'm not afraid," she insisted even as her nails dug
into the counter. Her heart hammered against her ribs.
She couldn't seem to catch her breath. He was so very
close.

"You look scared to death," he said, his eyes
darkly watchful. "As though you've never been
kissed. As though—"

The rest remained unspoken. He loomed over her,
big and hard and utterly male. His lips brushed hers,
startlingly gentle, warm, persuasive. She gave a soft,
feminine gasp of surprise and helpless pleasure. It was
all the invitation Mac needed. In one smooth motion,
he gathered her in his arms and took her mouth fully.

She had been kissed before, she had…she had…she had…

Sabrina struggled to remember that even as she confronted the stark truth that she had never been kissed like this. Never with such infinite care mingling with unfettered domination. Spasms of delight rippled through her all the way down her spine and beyond to make her toes actually curl in her shoes. She could do nothing but cling to the man who controlled her with tender strength, one big hand cupping the back of her head, holding her still for a sensual invasion that ripped away all pretense and left her buffeted by a storm of raw need she could scarcely credit.

When at last he raised his head, his own breathing was harsh and his eyes looked hungrier than ever. "Lady," he growled deep in his throat, "you ought to come with a warning label."

Sabrina shook her head dumbly, trying in vain to clear it. She could barely understand what had happened, much less what he was saying. Her hands were raised, the palms flattened against the hard wall of his chest, but she wasn't making any effort to push him away. On the contrary, she unabashedly savored his heat and power. Unbidden, the image rose in her mind of what it would be like to explore him without barriers or inhibition. A shudder ran down her length, making her suddenly, almost painfully aware of her vulnerability.

"Me?" she murmured. Her voice sounded like a croak. She cleared her throat and tried again. "I think you have that backward. Let me go…please."

He hesitated just long enough for her to realize that she had absolutely no idea what she would do if he refused. He was by far the largest and strongest man she had ever known. He was in peak condition, and she already sensed that he was a man accustomed to taking what he wanted. The stark reality was that she couldn't stop him from doing anything he chose.

What he chose, at least for the moment, was to release her. He stepped back and inhaled deeply, all the while watching her. Quietly he said, "I'll take you home."

"That's not necessary." She spoke so quickly, she all but stumbled over the words.

A pulse leaped to life in his jaw. She watched it with unwilling fascination. "If you think for one moment that I'll let you go home by yourself, you're not half as smart as I'm beginning to suspect you are."

Sabrina's chin rose a telling notch. The look she shot him was pure defiance. "I'm smart enough to know when things are happening too fast."

His eyes swept over her, hot and unhindered. "You've got a temper. That's good."

"It is?" She couldn't hide her surprise.

His answer was a wry smile. He waited while she grabbed her purse, set the alarm and locked up. Reaching around her, he checked to make sure the door was secure. "Can't be too careful," he said when she looked at him quizzically.

"Thanks for reminding me."

He chuckled but said nothing more as he helped her into the pickup parked at the corner. She noticed absently that the vehicle was relatively new and surprisingly clean considering that it was usually on a construction site.

"Where do you live?" he asked as he settled behind the wheel.

She told him, silently giving thanks that she had moved out of her father's plush town house. The apartment she was subletting from a cooking-school friend was nice enough, but it gave no hint whatsoever of her background. That was exactly as she wanted it.

Mac drove sedately, for him. He popped a cassette in the tape deck and let Pavarotti fill the silence. Either Sabrina was the least talkative woman he'd ever met or she was as befuddled by what was happening between them as he was. Grimly, he hoped the latter was true. She confused him and he couldn't remember the last time that had happened. He liked women, he really did. They were great for sharing pleasure with. Beyond that, he'd never considered and he wasn't about to now. His life was too busy, too demanding and too well-ordered to complicate it with a woman who was more than a bed partner. If that stance wasn't particularly enlightened, too bad.

He sent a spearing glance in Sabrina's direction. Her profile was as perfect as the rest of her. Unbidden, the memory of what her mouth felt like surged through him. He cursed under his breath and tightened his hands on the wheel.

"Is something wrong?" she asked in that slightly breathless voice that was driving him nuts.

"Yeah, but don't worry about it." He brought the

pickup to a stop in front of a modest brownstone on a quiet residential street in what he was relieved to see was an okay neighborhood. There were even a few trees along the curb, none of them very old but still a good indication that people were taking care of things.

With the engine off, he got out and moved to open the passenger-side door for her. In the back of his mind, he noticed that she didn't look surprised. She was used to courtesies that had all but vanished from their world.

He escorted her up the short flight of stone steps to the front door and waited while she got out her key. She turned it in the lock, then looked at him hesitantly. "I have an early day tomorrow."

"So do I." He bent down and touched his mouth to hers in the barest caress. If he allowed himself anything more, he risked pressing her for something she obviously wasn't ready to give. Straightening, he took a deep breath and looked into luminous violet eyes. "I'll call you."

He waited until she was inside and he saw lights come on in the third-floor apartment. For just a moment, he glimpsed her at the window, a slender arm raised to draw the curtains.

With a deep sigh, he headed for the truck. He was tired but already knew he wasn't likely to sleep well. Sabrina Giacanna got to him in some way he wasn't prepared for and didn't know what to do about. Even now, he wanted her so much he ached from it. Mild concern stirred in him at the thought that, if he let her, she could have real power over him. Not that he would ever allow that to happen. She was beautiful, all right, and sexy as hell, but she was also a startling combination of passion and innocence. He would need to tread carefully.

His thoughts shifting toward pleasant anticipation, Mac eased the truck back into traffic. He was preoccupied enough not to notice the dark sedan parked across the street from the brownstone, nor did he see the man seated in it put a cell phone to his ear, wait a moment and begin speaking.

Chapter 2

"It's no trouble at all," Sabrina said. "You just give Jenny a hug for me and don't worry about a thing."

She listened, making reassuring murmurs, then said, "Honestly, Sylvia, I'd be very upset if you *didn't* ask me." She laughed softly. "Besides, the truth is, it was fun. You and Joseph may yet convince me to go into the restaurant business full-time."

The other woman chuckled, relaxing as much as a mother with a sick child could, now that she knew there would be no problem getting coverage at work. "My sweet husband said you did a fabulous job yesterday. In fact, he went on and on about your pepper and crab bisque so much I could be a little jealous if I weren't so grateful."

"It's your recipe," Sabrina reminded her. "Tell your better half I just followed the directions. In fact,

I'll tell him myself this afternoon.'' She paused a moment, then asked, ''Did Joseph mention anything else?''

''He gave me the full rundown, but I have to admit I wasn't listening a hundred percent. I knew everything would be great with you there.''

Sabrina breathed a little sigh of relief. Joseph hadn't mentioned Mac to his wife. If he had said anything to his wife, it hadn't gone any further. Yet.

''Seriously,'' Sylvia said, ''you're a natural. It's the Giacanna genes. Every generation they produce women who are fabulous cooks.'' She laughed. ''And finally we can even get paid for it. Are you really thinking about coming into the business?''

''I'm more at the stage of thinking about thinking about it. So much has happened lately, I just need some time to adjust.''

It was Sylvia's turn to be reassuring. ''I know you've been in a tough situation, hon, but it will all work out. Your father just has to understand that you have your own life to live.''

''He wasn't being very understanding about it the last time I talked to him.''

''That's because of who he is...what he is. He's used to calling all the shots. He probably needs some time, too, to realize that you're not a little girl anymore.''

''Maybe you're right,'' Sabrina said, although she remained doubtful. Her last conversation with her father had been anything but encouraging. Her decision to move out had angered him to the point where he had actually tried to forbid it. As though a twenty-five-year-old woman didn't have the right to decide where and how she was going to live. It sounded incredible in this day and age, but Sabrina knew all too well that the rules that applied for most people didn't necessarily hold for Rourk Talveston's daughter.

She hung up a short time later and glanced at the clock. Joseph was seeing to the morning's shopping with Sylvia's detailed instructions in hand so she had a few more hours before she needed to be at the restaurant. She could use that time to take care of some errands and generally get herself in order. A quick look in the bathroom mirror made her grimace. There were dark shadows under her eyes and her usually pale skin looked completely washed out, but what could she expect after only a few hours of sleep broken by bouts of tossing and turning?

Mac had said that he would call her, but she'd realized belatedly that he didn't have her phone number. He'd never asked for it, maybe because he just assumed she was in the book or maybe because he was just being polite when he'd dropped her off. Whatever the case, she had decided during the interminable hours of the night that they really weren't suited to each other. She was too quiet and unassertive, which some people mistook for timidity but really wasn't. It was just that she had her own way of coming around to things, and she was going through a difficult time right now that made her vulnerable, which made her think it was definitely not good to be hanging around a man like Mac Donnelly. Except she had to be honest and admit that she didn't really know what kind of man he was, aside from the obvious, drop-dead gorgeous, incredibly masculine...and guarded. She definitely knew he was cautious because of how little he had revealed of a personal nature and because she was a private person herself, so she had no trouble recognizing it in another.

She was rambling again, her thoughts turning over and over but always coming back to Mac. He'd been with the same company for ten years, which meant he must have been in his early to mid-twenties when he started. From their conversation the previous night, she'd learned he was intelligent, well-read and he liked opera, all of which made it clear he didn't fit any stereotypes about construction workers. But then who did? If she'd had her wits about her last evening, she would have asked more questions about his family, but she'd been too busy deflecting his own about hers, which when she thought about it was kind of funny. Except she didn't really feel like laughing just now. She was too busy wondering if she would see him again.

Probably not, she decided by the time she let herself out of the apartment and headed for the subway. No doubt Mac Donnelly had better things to do than pursue a woman who got all flustered over one kiss and didn't even invite him up for coffee.

Emerging aboveground at the end of her ride, she paused for a moment to feel the sun on her face. New York was having a beautiful spring, people were actually smiling at each other, and there was an air of confidence and purpose that had been missing for a while. She'd never really thought of herself as a city person despite having spent so much of her life in one or another of them, but she had to admit the Big Apple was growing on her.

Her step was quick as she walked the few blocks from the subway, but it slowed as she came within sight of the excavation next to the restaurant. Dust rose from the immense hole, trailing in the path of rumbling machinery. Men seemed to be everywhere. To the untutored eye, it probably all looked very mysterious, but Sabrina had no trouble recognizing that more footings were being poured. She stopped, watching with interest as she realized that the men were laying a complete foundation mat rather than the separate footings that were more commonly used in this part of the country. The soil analysis must have turned up a potential problem. Put a skyscraper on top of fill without compensating properly and there could be all sorts of difficulties, if not outright dangers. Whoever was running this project for Century apparently had foreseen that and taken steps to avoid the problem. A vague half memory flitted through her mind, something about overhearing her father on the phone hearing him say something angrily about Century and its CEO. But the recollection was so fragmentary that she let it go.

Besides, she had far more immediate matters on her mind. Mac was down there somewhere. If she tried, she could probably spot him since he was significantly bigger than the other men. Pride stopped her, but it was touch-and-go for a moment. Annoyed with herself, she went into the restaurant and headed straight for the kitchen, determined to concentrate strictly on work.

For several hours, she succeeded. The lunch crowd was even larger than at dinner. There was no time to think of anything except the rush of incoming orders. Fortunately, the kitchen staff was a top-notch team that readily followed Sabrina's lead. There was a rhythm to their efforts that brought order to what easily could have been chaos.

All the same, by the time lunch was over Sabrina was glad to take a break before beginning preparations for dinner. She carried a couple of chairs out back, plopped down in one, put her feet up on the other, shut her eyes and tilted her face to the afternoon sun.

That was how Mac found her, sitting in the golden light, the soft breeze stirring the baby-fine curls of her hair, thick lashes resting on damask-smooth cheeks. For a long moment, he was content just to look at her. He'd spent a largely sleepless night because of her, but couldn't seem to mind. Besides, he hoped to spend many more the same way, although for much more enjoyable reasons.

Smiling slightly at that, he took a step closer and said, "Slacking off?"

Her eyes flew open. She gasped softly and sat up with a thump that rocked the chairs onto their back legs, which wiggled perilously, on the verge of tipping over altogether and taking her with them.

Mac lunged. He swept Sabrina into his arms the

instant before the chairs fell. She let out a little scream
that was cut off the moment her feet left the ground.
Those incredible violet eyes filled with a mingling of
feminine wariness and curiosity he found so very difficult to resist.

No, impossible. Even as he knew he should put her
down, he continued holding her. Carefully, remembering her apprehension the night before, he bent his
dark head and lightly touched his mouth to hers. She
stiffened, and for just a moment he thought she meant
to resist. But instead her body relaxed, molding to his,
her lips parted and she made a soft sound in the back
of her throat that threatened to drive him straight over
the edge.

He deepened the kiss, tasting her fully. Holding her
high against his chest with the sun pouring over them
both and the cacophonous life of the city going on
heedlessly, he forgot all else. Her arms twined around
the thick column of his neck, her fingers tangling in
his hair. She turned slightly, pressing closer, and ten-
tatively met the probing surge of his tongue with her
own.

Savage need ripped through him. He groaned and
tore his mouth away, only to trace a line of fire down
her slim throat then up again, returning to her lips with
even greater hunger. Holding her easily, he fought the
wild temptation to carry her the few hundred yards to
his office trailer and lock the world away.

All that stopped him was the high, piercing shrill of
a steam whistle finally penetrating his consciousness.
He looked up, dimly aware that the sound had been

going on for several minutes. His first thought was that something was wrong on the site, but he quickly spied the two men in the cab of a parked mixer, grinning broadly at the show they had just interrupted.

Mac cursed under his breath. He turned and set Sabrina down carefully, shielding her in front of him, then shot a look over his shoulder at the men that sent them rushing out of the cab and back to work. There was some satisfaction in that, although he didn't doubt part of their haste was eagerness to report what the boss had been up to.

Grimacing, he touched a hand to Sabrina's pale cheek. "You ought to be more careful."

Startled, she looked at him and touched her fingers to her lips. "Yes, I should."

"I meant about the chair."

"Chair? Oh, that." Belatedly, she murmured, "Thank you."

Her good manners annoyed him. He wanted her at least as bewildered and uncertain as he was. The temptation to kiss her again was very strong. He shoved his hands into the pockets of his jeans and said, "How about a movie tonight?"

Sabrina blinked once, then again and took a deep breath. All she had to do was say no. Or maybe, no, thank you. Or, gee, I'd like to but I'm really busy and—

"A movie would be fine."

Oh, great, now she'd really gone and done it. Wasn't there some rule book she was supposed to be following? Something about making the guy ask well in advance and not being easy? Where was she when the really important information got passed out?

He gave her one of those long, slow looks that made her bones melt, and grinned. "I'll pick you up at ten o'clock."

Joseph was at the back door when Sabrina returned to the kitchen. He didn't even pretend not to have been watching. The look on his face made Sabrina flush.

"You say he knows your father?"

She shut her eyes, prayed for patience—and for the right answer. "I didn't say that...exactly."

Joseph scowled. "Then perhaps I should enlighten him." He took a step toward the door as though intending to go after Mac.

"No!" Sabrina grabbed hold of his arm. "There's no need for that. For heaven's sake, I'm twenty-five years old. I moved out on my own to get away from this kind of thing."

"All the same—"

"No!" she said it even more forcefully. "I mean it, Joseph. If you do this, I'll walk out of here. One domineering, overprotective man in my life is enough. I don't need another."

He hesitated. Slowly, the scowl gave way to a slight smile. He glanced again in the direction Mac had gone. Amusement danced in his eyes. "All right. Sabrina, I understand how you feel. No more men like that." His smile deepened.

"What's so funny?" she asked suspiciously. He was giving in too easily.

"Oh, nothing, nothing at all." He was almost laughing.

Understanding dawned. She was a little slow sometimes when it came to the way men's minds worked. "You think Mac is like that."

"Well..."

"I wouldn't be attracted to him if he was."

"Of course you wouldn't." If he strained any harder to hold in his laughter, he was going to hurt himself.

"I like sensitive, caring men who respect women as competent equals."

"Nothing wrong with that," Joseph agreed, bending over slightly and holding his chest.

"Oh, stop it! If you break a rib, Sylvia will blame me."

He waved a hand in a vain attempt to reassure her. "No, I'm fine, really...it's just..."

She waited, thoroughly disgusted, until he was able to continue. "Just what?"

Joseph wiped a tear from the corner of his eye. "Men can be a little more complicated than you seem to think."

"I never said men were superficial. It would be really sexist to think that."

"Hmm, yes, well, all I'm saying is that it's possible to genuinely respect women but still feel a need to protect them from a world that isn't always what it should be."

"I don't need anyone to protect me," Sabrina insisted. "I'm perfectly capable of taking care of my-self."

"You be sure to explain that to Mac Donnelly," Joseph said right before he started laughing again.

Thoroughly disgruntled, Sabrina ignored him—as best she could—and got down to work on dinner. After a while, he went away but throughout the rest of the afternoon and evening, every time Joseph saw her he grinned. It wasn't until Mac arrived, on the dot at ten o'clock, that Joseph suddenly grew serious. He looked Mac up and down, nodded as though having confirmed something to his own satisfaction and said, "Sabrina is my cousin."

Hurrying to greet Mac and hopefully head off any confrontation between the two men, Sabrina heard her name and froze. But a quick glance at Mac revealed that he didn't seem at all perturbed.

"I figured something like that," he said as he and Joseph shook hands.

Joseph nodded. He and Mac let their arms drop, but continued to look right at each other. "Big family?" Mac asked.

"Big enough," Joseph replied.

Mac nodded thoughtfully. "There's a lot to be said for family."

"I'm glad you feel that way. How about yours?"

"I'm the oldest of five," Mac said. "All boys."

"Your brothers work construction?"

Mac nodded again. "Also my father and uncles."

Joseph seemed pleased. "That's good. Families should work together."

"There's a lot to be said for that, too."

They continued eyeing each other and nodding, until Sabrina had all she could take. Stepping between them, she murmured, "This is great, but we don't want to miss the movie."

"What are you seeing?" Joseph asked.

Sabrina shot him a quelling glance that he ignored. Mac didn't seem to mind answering. He even added, "It's rated PG-13."

"Oh, for God's sake—"

"Mac's just showing respect," Joseph interrupted. He frowned at her. "You should appreciate that." Both men looked at her chidingly.

She took a deep breath, let it out slowly and went to get her jacket. When she returned, the two were deep in conversation about soccer, but they broke it off politely.

"Have a good evening," Joseph said as he opened the door for them.

Mac nodded and took Sabrina's arm. As they walked toward the corner, he said, "Nice guy, your cousin."

"He's a little old-fashioned." She wasn't going to say anything more than that, she absolutely wasn't. If the two of them wanted to behave like throwbacks to another era, looking after the little woman, they could just go right ahead and do it.

"Nothing wrong with that," Mac replied.

A sudden thought occurred to her. "He didn't say anything more to you, did he?"

"About what?"

"Family... Joseph's very big on family, loves to rattle on about it." Had he said something to Mac about her father when she wasn't there to hear it? She didn't think Joseph would do something like that, but all that male camaraderie had her shaken up.

"We talked about soccer."

"Do you play?"

"Now and again." The modest shrug of those impossibly broad shoulders suggested there was more to it. "My family lived in Ireland for a while after Ma died. I picked it up there."

"I'll bet you're good...at soccer." She added the last part hastily.

He shot her a quick look. The color in her cheeks must have been obvious because he chuckled. "There's a game this weekend. Want to come?"

She managed a smile that she hoped hid her nervousness. "Sure."

With an effort, Mac made himself look away. They were crossing a street; it would be a good idea to pay some attention to the traffic even if that simple task seemed to stretch whatever was left of his mental capabilities. She was so damn beautiful, and the way she blushed at the simplest things drove him crazy. She couldn't possibly be as innocent as she seemed... could she? Meeting Joseph again had really made him wonder. He liked her cousin, they understood each other, but he'd never dated a woman from a big, protective, old-fashioned family. That the woman in question also provoked the hardest, hottest, most unrelenting lust he'd ever experienced made the situation interesting, to say the least.

He would have to remember to warn his brothers about her before the weekend. All he needed was for one of them to let drop what he really did for a living. There would be enough trouble to deal with just because he was bringing a woman to the game. He'd never done that before and knew he would be in for some serious kidding, but he couldn't regret the impulse that had made him invite her. The plain truth was that he wanted to be with Sabrina Giacanna any way he could. If that meant maneuvering around her family and his, then that was just what he would do.

Halfway through the movie, which didn't make much of an impression on him but which Sabrina seemed to enjoy, it occurred to him that he'd never gone to this much effort for a woman before. He was still mulling that over when they left the theater. So much so that he didn't notice the man in the driver's seat of the dark sedan parked across the street. The man who, seeing them go by, checked his watch and jotted something in a notebook before swinging the car into traffic to follow at a discreet distance.

"A girl?" Seamus Donnelly finished off his hamburger, wiped his fingers on a paper napkin and frowned at his brother. "You're bringing a girl on Saturday?"

"Woman, not girl," Mac said. He shoved away what remained of his own lunch and propped his feet up on the marble desk that dominated one end of the corner office on the fiftieth floor of the building that housed the headquarters of Century Construction and its several subsidiaries. "Don't you read those memos Personnel sends out about politically correct language?"

"No," Seamus said cheerfully, "and since when did you? So who is she?"

"Her name is Sabrina Giacanna," Mac said cautiously.

"Italian. Sounds good."

"Yeah, well, there are a few complications with that, big family and all, but never mind. The thing is, I haven't exactly been upfront with her."

His brother's dark eyebrows, copies of his own, rose. "How so?"

"She doesn't know who I am."

"She doesn't know you're Mac Donnelly?"

"No, of course she knows that. She just doesn't know that I run Century."

"What does she think you do?"

Mac grimaced. Here it came. "She thinks I'm foreman on a mixer crew."

Seamus's mouth worked. "I see…hell, no, I don't. Why would she think that?"

"Because I let her think it. I'm tired of being with women who can figure my net worth faster than I can. Sabrina's just a nice girl from a big family that really cares about her and still has actual values."

Seamus's eyes, the same blue with touches of gray, widened. "Uh-oh, this sounds serious. What does she look like?"

"You'll see on Saturday."

"Gimme a hint, just so I won't make a total fool out of myself."

"You'll do that anyway. She's...beautiful."

"You want to elaborate on that?"

"She looks like she stepped out of a Renaissance painting, all right? You satisfied now?"

His brother laughed. "No way. So what does this gorgeous Italian chick with the big family do for a living?"

"She's a chef," Mac admitted grudgingly.

"You mean she cooks?"

"I'm really glad I paid for that expensive education of yours."

Seamus laughed. "You've got to admit, that's not your usual style. Big family, drop-dead gorgeous and cooks. I don't know, bro, you better be serious about this girl—sorry, *woman*—or you and me maybe gonna have a little one-on-one."

He said it lightly, but there was a gleam in Seamus's eyes that Mac didn't mistake. Slowly, unfolding his full height, he stood and looked down at his brother.

"No," he said quietly, "we're not."

Seamus whistled softly. "That's the way of it?"

Mac nodded. "That's the way."

A grin spread slowly across Seamus's chiseled features. He got out of the chair, punched his brother lightly in the shoulder and said, "Any chance I get to tell the others?"

The look Mac shot him said it all. Seamus was still laughing as the office door closed behind him.

Chapter 3

Clods of dirt flew up into the air as bodies smashed together with a sickening thud. Sabrina squeezed her eyes shut and swallowed hard. It was just a game, just a game, just a game. If she repeated that often enough, she might even believe it.

Some game. The Donnelly brothers—all six of them—apparently played to win. That they happened to be evenly split between opposing sides didn't seem to make any difference. No quarter was asked, or given.

Watching the seeming chaos on the grassy field, Sabrina had no trouble picking out Mac or his brothers. Introduced to them just before the game began, she'd been confused and not a little overwhelmed at finding herself surrounded by so many big, hard-muscled, grinning males. Mac had kept an arm draped over her shoulders in a gesture she wanted to think of as sweetly protective, but had to recognize as blatantly possessive. It only seemed to increase his brothers' amusement, although she had to admit they all be-haved impeccably, from Eamon, who was only a cou-ple of years younger than Mac, on down the line through Padraic and the twins, Sean and Baird, to Sea-mus, who at twenty-two was the "baby" of the fam-ily.

Some baby and some family. Not one of them was under six feet three inches, and they were all in peak condition. Eamon and Seamus had the same midnight black hair as Mac, although they both wore theirs somewhat shorter. Padraic, Sean and Baird all had varying shades of gold shot through with red. Their features were similar enough to mark them as brothers even to the least observant eye, yet each man was unique. And each, she couldn't help but notice, was shockingly handsome, although none was quite so compelling as Mac.

Which just might have had something to do with the number of young women who seemed to have de-cided that this was the perfect day to wander into the park and watch a soccer game. Several of them were jumping up and down, cheering enthusiastically, just as Mac kicked a hard, straight drive into the opposing goal.

Sabrina glared at the silly, squealing things, but they were oblivious, too caught up in the heady pleasure of watching the Donnelly men. However, her reaction didn't go completely unnoticed. A warm, masculine chuckle behind her made Sabrina turn suddenly.

The man who stood there was also very tall, with ebony hair lightly streaked with silver and a smile that was all too breathtakingly familiar. In his late fifties or perhaps even older, casually dressed in khakis and a pullover, he had rugged good looks that matched his unmistakable intelligence and humor.

Holding out his hand, he said, "You'd be Sabrina."

Her own hand was swallowed up in his, yet his touch was gentle and careful. Looking into his eyes—the same startlingly blue shade as Mac's—she couldn't help but smile. "Forgive me, but are you the uncle or the father?"

His laughter rumbled. "Ah, lass, keep looking like that and I dare say you'd be forgiven anything. It's the father I am. Quinn's the name. My brother, Kane, is—" He caught himself suddenly. "Off on a job. Now what's this I hear about you being able to cook?"

"Did Mac tell you that?" Her cheeks warmed as she wondered what else he'd seen fit to mention to his father. In the not quite week since she and Mac had met, they'd seen each other every evening for dinner or a movie or both. And every evening he had escorted her back to her apartment, staying only long enough for a cup of coffee. The few kisses they had shared left her dazed and yearning for more. Her sleep was ragged, filled with dreams of him from which she woke trembling and shocked by the vividness of her own imagination.

"He said you're a terrific chef," Quinn told her.

"Of course, he thinks chili straight out of the can is a perfectly fine meal, so I'm withholding judgment until I get a chance to try some of your cooking for myself."

"I can promise you to do better than that," she said with a laugh. Another cheer went up and she glanced over her shoulder, grimacing as she saw Mac hit the ground. He seemed to go down awfully hard. When he didn't get up right away, she took a quick step toward the field.

Quinn took hold of her arm gently and drew her back. "He's fine, lass. Takes a whole lot more than that to keep Mac down." True to his father's words, Mac rose lithely, dusted himself off with a grin and went straight back into the game. The cheering section liked that a whole lot and didn't hesitate to let him know it.

"I didn't realize so many women were soccer fans," Sabrina muttered.

Quinn's eyes crinkled. "The lads were saying the other night it'd be time to change fields again soon."

"Change fields?"

"Aye, it's always the same. They find a good place to play, then one or two of the fairer sex happen by, word spreads and before too long—well, you can see for yourself. It gets distracting after a while so they move on."

"Must be tough." She was being ungracious and knew it. Abashed, she said, "I have cousins who play soccer. Perhaps they could suggest a place."

Quinn nodded thoughtfully. His gaze did not waver

from her despite the continued action on the field. "Do you play yourself?"

She shook her head, the image of herself racing down a soccer field being startling, to say the least. Her father never would have allowed it.

"You're not interested in sports?" Quinn probed.

"Oh, it isn't that. I like to swim and to—" She hesitated, aware that she might reveal more about herself than she really wanted to but too weary of watching her every word to stop herself. "Ride."

Quinn's eyes lit. "Ah, now, riding's a fine thing. I made sure all my boys learned. Mac has a fine seat. Why, when he's—"

It was the older Donnelly's turn to break off. Sabrina watched, puzzled, as a slight flush touched his lean cheeks. "That is, when he's riding, you'd think man and horse were one."

"I had no idea he rode. He never mentioned it." She frowned slightly, thinking of the faint but growing unease she felt over how little Mac really did say about himself. She knew—or at least she thought—he had grown up in New York except for the several years he'd lived in Ireland. He had said little about his education and she was hesitant about asking, for she sensed his pride was fierce and she didn't want to embarrass him in any way. Besides, he was clearly highly intelligent and well-informed in all regards. They had fascinating discussions about everything under the sun, yet very little of a personal nature was ever mentioned. Of course, she was hardly in a position to complain about a lack of candor when she had so deliberately misled him about her own identity.

"Something wrong, lass?" Quinn's voice was a low rumble, drawing her out of her thoughts.

A little startled, she managed a smile. "Not at all." Turning toward the field, she asked, "Who's winning?"

"Mac's team is, but only by one goal and the other side's giving him a good run."

"Your sons are very competitive, aren't they?"

Quinn laughed. At least, it started out as a laugh. Before long, he was practically gasping. Sabrina thought of Joseph and sighed. Lately, she seemed to have no end of ability in amusing men.

Wiping a tear from his eye, Quinn said, "I'm sorry, lass. You just took me by surprise there. Aye, you could call them competitive, all right." He started laughing again but caught himself. "Still and all, there's nothing they wouldn't do for each other. I'd wager your family's the same."

Sabrina thought of the boisterous, warm-hearted Giacannas and nodded. When it came to them, she always felt like a kid with her nose pressed up against the candy-store window. They would be appalled to know that and would do everything possible to assure her she truly was one of them, but Sabrina knew better. Life had left her isolated in many ways. Going out on her own was her first real effort to end that, but she still had no idea if it could work.

Since meeting Mac, she found herself hoping all the more that it would. With those hopes came a plethora of cautions about not expecting too much or assuming anything...or letting her heart overrule her head, which it was very much in danger of doing where he was concerned.

That same heart that was ramming against her ribs as Mac raced down the field, unusually fast and lithe for a man of his size, laughing as he evaded Sean's effort to block him, and finally kicking the ball in a hard, straight drive into the goal.

A roar went up, the deep, full-throated cheers of males drowning out the sidelines. The game was over. Mac's team had won and he looked pleased—although to be fair, they all did.

"They lost last week," Quinn said by way of explanation. "It evens out. Both sides are too well matched for one to win more than half the time."

"Did they ever think of playing on the same side?"

Quinn's eyes twinkled. "Aye, they did. But when they tried, they had a damn hard time finding anyone to play against them."

Sabrina could well believe it. The Donnelly men were a formidable bunch, yet she barely noticed the rest of them. All her attention was on Mac as he crossed the field to where she and his father were standing.

Streaked with sweat and dirt, powerful muscles rippling in his arms and chest, he reminded her of the very first time she saw him. There was something raw and primitive about Mac Donnelly, yet he was also a man of intelligence and refinement. Altogether, it was a heady combination that drew her irresistibly.

"I see you've met," Mac said, his eyes going from one to the other. He looked watchful, as always. As she did more and more lately, Sabrina wondered why.

"We have and I'll tell you now, she's much too good for you."

Sabrina flushed in surprise, her gaze darting to Quinn, but Mac only laughed. He draped an arm over her shoulders exactly as he had before, nestled her up against his hard length, and said, "Figured that out, did you? What's that Browning said? 'A man's reach should exceed his grasp, or what's a heaven for?'

"Aye," Quinn murmured, "but didn't he also say, 'Where my heart lies, let my brain lie also?'"

Mac chuckled. "I should know better than to quote poetry to my father. He's bound to have a comeback." Yet he seemed well pleased by the exchange, if a bit rueful.

Sabrina blinked and tried to decide what to make of it all. Big, hard, capable men who quoted poetry with the ease of sports statistics and seemed to take a fierce, loving pleasure in all life offered. Only one thing was clear to her—she was out of her depth and sinking fast.

"I need a shower." Mac released her, only to take hold of her hand, his big fingers curling around hers. "We'll be off then."

"She's promised to cook for us," Quinn called after them.

Mac looked back over his shoulder. "Didn't know what she was getting into, did she?"

"You might have warned me," Sabrina said when

they were in his truck, heading back toward her apartment. "Five brothers *and* your father. You could have said something."

"And spoil the surprise?" His teeth flashed whitely as he grinned. "What did you think of them?"

"Your brothers are a bit overwhelming," she said honestly. "So's your father, but he's...nice."

The elder Donnelly had startled her most of all. She sensed in him some of the same qualities of strength and determination that she knew in her own father, yet in Quinn they were leavened by gentleness and humor, attributes Rourk Talveston had never exhibited in his life.

Mac nodded. "He's a good one. Seen a lot of life, but never let it get him down." He paused, then added, "Except when my mother died. That was very bad. My uncle raised us for a while, until Da was all right again."

They had not talked of this link between them since their second evening together. Sabrina hesitated, aware that she was moving into uncharted ground. Softly, she said, "Do you remember your mother?"

"Very well. I was ten when she passed."

"What happened to her?"

"She got sick. Turned out she had a very rare heart disorder. There was nothing anyone could do."

"No transplant?" Sabrina murmured.

"They were only just starting up with that then. She was on the list. Her name didn't come up in time." A nerve flicked in his jaw, but his hands on the wheel were steady. It was an old pain and an old rage. He'd had a lot of practice dealing with both.

"What about your mother?" he asked without warning, although to be fair she should have seen it coming.

Sabrina took a deep breath. She had never spoken of this with anyone, not even her father. Her only knowledge of it came from the family attorney whom she'd confronted after girls at school taunted her with rumors.

Quietly, she said, "My mother was kidnapped and murdered." Before he could do more than look at her in astonishment, she added, "Thousands of people die violently every year, she was one of them. It happened just a few months after I was born."

"That's terrible." His voice was low and gentle. "Was the killer caught?"

"There were two of them and, yes, they were."

"Are they still in jail?" She saw the hard glint in his eyes and she shivered inwardly. He had no way of knowing that he was touching on dark, hidden shadows she had never allowed herself to examine too closely.

"They were killed in a prison brawl."

He nodded once, decisively. "That's good."

Sabrina nodded, too, glad that he was satisfied. For herself, she had long since accepted that she would never know whether the fight that killed her mother's slayers was real or merely a cover-up for two more murders. Her father would never discuss it with her and she had never been able to bring herself to broach the subject with him, as much from fear of what she would learn as from any other reason.

"Would you mind if I shower at your place?" he asked in what she knew was a deliberate change of subject. It worked very well. The painful thoughts eating at the edge of her mind were suddenly, almost shockingly swamped by the image of Mac standing naked in her shower, water sluicing over powerful muscles and bronzed skin.

"Uh, sure..." She sounded like one of those chipmunks on television. Clearing her throat, she tried again. "That would be fine."

He'd been inside her apartment before, but once again it struck him oddly. There was nothing particularly wrong with the comfortable, slightly dowdy furniture of no discernible style; it just didn't seem to fit Sabrina. He saw her in some place less cluttered, more defined, some place that had at least some sign of the things he knew by now that she really cared about— cooking, music, books.

She got fresh towels out of the closet and handed them to him without meeting his eyes. Mac hid a smile. He'd known suggesting the shower would unsettle her and had done it anyway on purpose, partly to distract her from the tragedy of her mother's death, which had shocked him profoundly, but also because he still couldn't believe that she was as innocent as she seemed. He found himself needing to keep testing that possibility, certain he had to be wrong yet wondering all the same.

Her cheeks were slightly flushed as he thanked her for the towels, taking them in the same hand that held his gym bag with its change of clothes. "I'll fix some lunch," she said and retreated down the narrow hallway to the kitchen.

Mac turned the taps on in the shower, stripped, then stepped under the nozzle. The initial rush of cold water made him grit his teeth, but he bore it as he always did, his clenched muscles not relaxing until the temperature rose and steam began to fill the small room. Lathering soap over his chest, he stopped for a moment as the scent of honeysuckle teased him. He'd picked up the bar without thinking and was paying for that carelessness now as a wave of hot, surging lust rocked him. Sabrina's skin carried the faintest hint of honeysuckle. The same soap he was holding had passed over her perfectly shaped breasts, rounded hips, slender thighs—

A curse broke from him. He dropped the bar back onto the side of the tub and reached outside the curtain for the soap he'd left there. A grimace twisted his hard mouth. Feeling jealous of a bar of soap was about as pathetic as it got, but then what did he expect, given the insane self-restraint he'd been exercising the past few days? Every evening, he'd left Sabrina with only a few kisses despite the nearly uncontrollable need to lay her down on the nearest horizontal surface and drive into her sweet, yielding body over and over until at least some fraction of the hard, raw need she provoked was eased.

His nights had become pure torture, his days little

better. He was alternately stunned, humbled and re-
sentful of what she did to him. In the back of his mind,
he kept thinking that if he just saw enough of her,
some of that impact would wear off and she would
start to seem more like the women he'd known before.
But that wasn't happening. Frustration was eating at
him, and there was going to have to be an end to it
soon.

He lingered long enough in the shower to finish
washing his hair, then toweled off quickly. Dressed in
clean khakis and a pullover, he combed his hair back
wet and secured it at the nape of his neck. He automatically tidied up the bathroom, dropping the towel
in the hamper and putting the rest of his clothes in his
bag. Emerging into the hall, he smelled something
very different from the honeysuckle but in its own way
almost as tantalizing. A wry smile eased the hard lines
of his face as he considered that Sabrina appealed to
all sorts of appetites.

He found her in the kitchen, a plain white apron
tied snugly around her hips and a slight frown creasing
her forehead as she concentrated on whatever it was
she was cooking. She'd kicked off her shoes and was
barefoot, as he'd noticed she preferred to be. Wisps of
honeyed hair drifted softly around her cheeks. She
flicked a strand away absently and kept frowning.

"Something wrong?" Mac asked.

She jumped a good half foot, dropped the spoon she
was holding and stared at him wide-eyed.

Mac grinned. "Forget I was here?"

The look she gave him suggested he must have

taken leave of his senses even to consider such a thing. She started to say something, caught herself, and instead picked up the spoon and resumed stirring. With her back to him again, she said, "Sorry, I tend to get a little foggy when I'm cooking."

"All that concentration?"

"I guess. Anyway, nothing's wrong. I thought I'd put in too much fennel but it's really fine."

Mac tried to think of all the dishes he knew that required fennel but came up blank. Still, whatever she was preparing smelled great.

The table beside the window was already set with white place mats edged with small yellow flowers, matching napkins and a brown crockery pitcher filled with white and yellow daisies. The dishes were plain white, solid and serviceable. Of everything in the apartment, that one small area seemed to fit with what he thought he knew of Sabrina. Staring at it, a sudden possibility occurred to him.

"Are you subleasing?" he asked as he accepted the wine bottle she held out along with the corkscrew and began opening it.

"Yes, I am, from a friend I knew at school."

He nodded, pleased that he'd figured it out, and pulled the cork loose. "That explains it." He caught himself the moment the words were out, but it was too late.

She ladled a thick soup into deep white bowls before replying. "Explains what?"

Mac hesitated, looking for the simplest way to undo the damage. He smiled and shrugged lightly. "Just that this place is fine, but it doesn't seem very much like you. How long have you been here?''

"About a month." She set down the ladle and looked at him closely. "You were going to say something else, weren't you?"

He gave her a who-me look that could have been patented, but she wasn't buying. Leaning against the counter, she continued watching him steadily. "You've done that before, caught yourself, and I've wondered why. Now I really want to know."

For just a moment he considered continuing to deny it, but decided there wasn't any point. She was too damn perceptive, at least where he was concerned. Later, he would have to sort out how he felt about that.

"It explains why I had trouble getting your phone number."

She nodded. "I meant to give it to you, but it turned out you already had it. I did wonder how you managed that, considering the phone is still in my friend's name."

He'd managed it by calling a top executive at the phone company who was only too happy to do a favor for the CEO of Century Construction. It was a few minutes' work to have all the numbers for Sabrina's building pulled then delegate a couple of line guys working in the neighborhood to figure out which went to her apartment.

None of which was consistent with being foreman on a mixer crew. Cautiously, he said, "A friend of mine works at the phone company."

"That explains it," Sabrina said lightly, mimicking his own words. She went back to ladling soup. "My friend will be back in the fall, so I'll have to find a place of my own. I should be looking, but I haven't gotten around to it yet."

It was on the tip of his tongue to suggest she let him help her look, then use that as an opportunity to get her a really good deal. He had markers he could pull in, favors done in full expectation all around that they would be reciprocated. He didn't know how much a fill-in chef made, but he was willing to bet it wasn't a fortune. Rents were sky-high, while the chances of her finding something she could both afford and feel comfortable in were practically nonexistent.

"Where did you live before?" he asked, trying to get a sense of what she was used to paying.

Sabrina set a basket of warm bread on the table. "Here and there. I was out of the country for a while, studying mainly in France and Italy. That was great, but my favorite was the summer I spent working in Ireland."

"You were cooking there?"

She nodded. "Down in the southwest. There's been a huge revival in Irish cuisine. Even the French are going there now to study and open restaurants."

"I didn't know that. It's been years since I was over."

"You ought to get back. It's wonderful there."

The thought of visiting Ireland again, with Sabrina at his side, had a definite appeal. He smiled at the thought, raised the spoon he'd filled to his mouth and found he'd just swallowed a bit of heaven.

"What is this?" he asked when he was able.

She laughed, obviously pleased by his reverent tone.

"I haven't named it yet, but it's made with a really good chicken stock, slices of apple and chicken sausage, fennel and a few other things."

"You invented this?"

She shrugged modestly and handed him the bread basket. "Most chefs come up with their own ideas. It's just part of the job."

"Maybe, but I don't think too many come up with anything this good." The game had left him hungry but he ate slowly, savoring the meal. He drew her into a longer talk about the cooking schools she'd gone to, and she did answer his questions, but he still couldn't shake the idea that she was considering her responses far more carefully than seemed to be warranted.

"You've traveled a lot," he observed as they were clearing up. He wondered if that accounted for the difference he sensed in her, if she was more of a mixture of cultures than he'd realized at first.

"I've been lucky that way," she said and busied herself with the dishes.

They worked in companionable silence until the job was done. As Sabrina dried her hands, she tried but failed to suppress a grin. "I don't suppose you read women's magazines?"

He was surprised. "No, can't say I do."

"Well, if you did, you'd know you just scored a ten on every Mr. Sensitivity quiz ever published."

"You're kidding." He was appalled and sounded it.

Sabrina laughed. "Sorry to be the one to break it to you, but helping to clean up after dinner, including actually putting the dishes away, guarantees you top spot."

"Really," he said as he wadded up the towel he'd been using and dropped it onto the counter. "In that case, maybe I'd better do something caveman to redeem myself."

She had just a moment to look startled before his hands closed on her shoulders and he drew her to him. His mouth was hot, hard and hungry. He devoured hers, nibbling at her lower lip, drawing it into his mouth to suck, tracing the curve of it with his tongue before stroking deeply, repeatedly. He felt her surprise and sudden tension, felt, too, when that changed abruptly as she made a soft, whimpering sound and molded to him.

He ran his hands down her slender back to cup the curve of her buttocks and lifted her against him. Her hips moved instinctively, wringing a groan from deep in his chest. He pressed her back against the counter, pulled her legs apart and hooked them over his hips, bringing them into even more shockingly intimate contact. Tearing his mouth from hers, he raked his teeth along her throat before pushing aside the edges of her blouse to give him access to her breasts. Holding her with one arm, he pulled the fragile barrier apart and gazed down at her. She was wearing a lace and silk bra that was little more than a transparent scrap.

Her nipples were puckered, straining against the thin fabric, the areolas a deep rose.

"Beautiful," he murmured and took her into his mouth, alternately suckling and licking first one nipple, then the other until even the slight barrier became intolerable. The soft, whimpering sounds that broke from her drove him close to madness, but some tiny remnant of reason remained. Enough for him to become suddenly aware of exactly what it was he was doing. His hand was on the waistband of her shorts. The button was already undone, the zipper lowered. He was reaching inside to—

He didn't know this woman. Not really. Not considering the doubts that kept circling in his mind every time she evaded a question, or gave a half answer, or simply looked away at a particular moment. The fact that he was concealing from her the truth about himself had stopped him from pursuing her too closely, but that no longer mattered. There was something about Sabrina Giacanna, something he couldn't figure out, that made him extremely cautious of her.

Or at least made his brain cautious. The rest of him was anything but.

He groaned and set her down slowly, the touch of her body all along his length only increasing the pulsating ache that had him teetering on the very edge of a complete loss of control. That had never happened to him, absolutely never. He had enjoyed women, often intensely, but he was always fully in control. The realization of how close he was to losing control strengthened his resolve.

Carefully, he drew together the edges of her blouse and took a step back. Inhaling a deep breath, he said, ''I didn't mean for that to get out of hand.''

Sabrina looked up at him dazedly. Her eyes were wide and luminous, dark with passion. Her full mouth was slightly swollen. A delicate flush stained her cheeks. Her breasts, just barely covered now, rose and fell rapidly. She started to speak, stopped, and stared at him for several more moments before abruptly realizing her condition. Her lips pressed tightly together. Quickly, she turned away and reordered her clothes. Her hands were shaking and he could see the faint tremors that racked her.

Remorse filled him. He was about to reach out, seeking only to comfort her, when she realized his intent and shook her head. ''No, don't.'' She looked away from him, focusing on the far wall, and swallowed hard. ''I think you'd better go.''

His immediate instinct was to refuse; the thought of leaving her in such a state tore at him, but he also knew he couldn't stay without returning right to where they had been moments before. He needed time to come to terms with his doubts about Sabrina but also to decide how to tell her the truth about himself, for there was no longer any question in his mind that he had to do exactly that.

''I'll call you tomorrow,'' he said when he was at the door.

She still wouldn't look at him, but she did just barely nod. He held on to that as he headed for home and what promised to be a very long night.

Chapter 4

"I'm sorry, Mr. Donnelly, but you committed to the meeting a month ago. If I'd realized that you'd changed your mind, I would have notified city hall."

Mac slumped back in his desk chair, stared up at the ceiling and sighed. He'd completely forgotten about the business roundtable the mayor had scheduled for that afternoon. It was one of the duties his position required of him, a too-big, too-long, too-public meeting where nothing of any consequence would get done but where there would be plenty of photo opportunities. He hated that sort of thing, but he also recognized that it was just another part of the game he played to win. If occasionally he had to do things he didn't particularly like, that was the price of admission.

Under normal circumstances, he would have steeled

himself and gone, but he'd forgotten what normal felt like since meeting a certain blond witch who had him tied up in knots.

"It's not your fault, Liz," he said tiredly. He glanced at the motherly woman who had been with him since the day he opened for business. Liz Healey was in her late fifties and looked like everyone's favorite neighbor. She'd stayed home for years raising four kids, then went back into the workforce when it was time to send them to college, earned her M.B.A. by going to school at night, and had been known to bring fresh-baked cookies to the office. She also had a steel-trap mind, a six-figure salary and as good a knowledge of Century Construction as anyone who wasn't male, six foot plus and surnamed Donnelly.

"Anything else I've forgotten?" Mac asked, only half facetiously. He'd lain awake most of the previous night, trying to decide what to do about Sabrina, only to rise before dawn in a largely fruitless effort to get some work done. Now he figured he might as well go to the mayor's coffee klatch. He wasn't doing anyone any good where he was.

Liz frowned slightly, gave him the once-over and said, "Care to talk about it?"

He shrugged, rising as he did so, and reached for the suit jacket that was hanging on the back of the chair. The offer was tempting, but he was a private man who was inclined to solve his problems himself.

"Thanks," he said, "but no. I'd better get going."

Liz nodded, not offended in any way, but he was

aware that she continued to watch him with some concern as he left the office.

He used the time on the trip downtown to make some phone calls and catch up on paperwork. By the time his driver dropped him off in front of city hall, he felt more in gear and ready to focus on the business at hand. Striding up the wide stone steps in front of the Greco-style building, he resolutely turned his thoughts to what lay ahead.

A mayoral assistant Mac vaguely recognized saw him as soon as he came through the main doors. "This way, Mr. Donnelly," the young man said, ushering him around the security checkpoint. Mac nodded, letting himself be shepherded along to the second-floor conference room he'd been in all too many times before. So far as he'd ever been able to determine, nothing of importance happened in cavernous chambers with baroque ceiling murals and oil paintings of long-vanished city leaders. About a dozen guests were already present, grouped around the silver coffee service tended by a liveried waiter. Mac exchanged nods with the earlier arrivals. There were no surprises; he recognized them all. New York was really a very small town, at least when it came down to those who held genuine power.

People continued to filter in until there were perhaps fifty gathered in the room that could have held three times that. Only three women were in attendance, but the men present were drawn from a wide sprinkling of ethnic groups. Still, as a group they all—the women included—had far more in common than could ever differentiate them.

They shared the ineffable aura of success visible in small but telling ways: subtly superb tailoring that could never come off a rack; body language that spoke of alert intelligence and confidence; and even a certain camaraderie despite the fact that many had been—and would be again—competitors. They understood one another, and among themselves at least they could drop some of the pretenses maintained for more public consumption.

The doors at the far end of the chamber were closed and the conference proceeded. To Mac's surprise, there was actually some discussion of substance. Not much, to be sure, but at least enough to make him feel as though he hadn't entirely wasted his time. At the meeting's conclusion, the doors were reopened and the city hall press corps trundled in. The mayor read a statement clearly drafted before-the-fact but perfectly acceptable nonetheless, the questions were no more inane than usual, flashbulbs popped, video cameras whirred, and that was that.

But not quite. Mac was on his way out the door, glad it was over and already busy thinking about what else he needed to do that day when a tall, slender man stepped into his path. He smiled, put out a hand, and said, "Rourk Talveston. I believe we've met a time or two."

Mac stopped, looked at the man directly and frowned. Rourk Talveston was only an inch or two shorter than Mac, which was still taller than average.

He had the lean build of a runner, hair now more silver than brown, and eyes of a disconcerting purple hue. In his late fifties, Talveston ruled over a construction empire rivaled only by Mac's own company. The two men had gone head-to-head repeatedly over the past decade, but had given each other wide berth when their paths inevitably crossed at charity functions and other events. Now suddenly Talveston seemed inclined to change that. Mac was instantly suspicious and on the alert.

All the same, he offered his own hand and the two shook. The courtesies observed, they took a step back and studied each other. Mac was coldly wary but Talveston actually looked...pleased. A smile pulled at the corners of his mouth and his eyes were almost warm.

"Great job you did on the West Side development," he said.

Mac managed to restrain a snort of disbelief but just barely. Talveston Enterprises and Century Construction had fought a long and bitter battle for control of that especially plum job whose total value ran into the billions. Mac had won through a combination of ruthless determination, ice-cold tactics and unrelenting pressure, but the race had been very close.

"Thanks," he said, continuing to eye Talveston with the attention he would have given a particularly hungry anaconda. "Your Battery project looks to be coming along nicely."

The older man shrugged modestly. "Can't complain. We ran into a problem a few months back when it looked as though we might have hit a graveyard.

Thank God it turned out to be a run-of-the-mill murder, no more than a decade ago.''

"Thank God," Mac echoed, only half facetiously. He, too, had known the frustration—and cost—of a job brought to a standstill when the archaeologists descended. As much as he appreciated historical importance and all that, it wasn't something he would wish even on Rourk Talveston.

"His Honor was in fine form today," Talveston said as he began walking with Mac toward the exit.

His mind furiously considering what the man could possibly want, Mac answered, "He usually is."

"True enough. You'll be supporting him next year then?"

Was party politics what this was about then? Was Talveston taking on fund-raising for the mayor? Campaign solicitation was a bit blatant for the head of a company that benefited greatly from city contracts, but it certainly wasn't unheard of. It was usually just handled with a bit more delicacy.

"Of course," Mac said. The current occupant of the mayor's office was actually doing a good enough job to make running against him unappealing and fruitless. He was likely to have an easy reelection campaign. "Last I heard, he was unopposed."

Talveston laughed. He seemed genuinely pleased. "That's a pragmatic answer if I ever heard one." He stopped walking, turned and looked right at Mac. "But then you're a pragmatic man, aren't you, Donnelly? Nothing else would have gotten you to the top so fast."

"I'm not at the top," Mac said quietly.

Talveston's smile deepened. "You will be in another year or so, maybe sooner. We both know that. I'm going to have to get used to Talveston Enterprises being number two in this town."

Somehow, Mac didn't think second best was something Rourk Talveston would ever get used to. They paused at the top of the stone steps just outside the main doors where they were surrounded by people on their way in and out of city hall. Down below at the curb, a line of limousines waited. Bright sunlight washed through the canyons of the city, turning them golden. Looking up, Mac saw an entire cloud bank reflected in the glass panes of a nearby office building. The sight brought an unexpected tightness to his throat as he realized, not for the first time, the deep affection he had for this turbulent, lusty city.

"Does that mean you've given up the idea of acquiring us?" Mac asked pleasantly. For two years, he had waged a sporadic battle against Talveston's attempts to acquire his company. Nothing was ever said openly, no one ever acknowledged being behind the effort, but Mac was sure he knew who was doing it all the same. Only Rourk Talveston had the capital, the savvy and the motivation.

Now the man made no attempt to deny it. "Your strategy to hold us off has been excellent, we both know that. The fact is, I've come to the conclusion that I'd prefer a more amicable relationship. What would you say to coming up to my place in Greenwich—maybe spend the weekend? It would give us a chance to get to know each other better.''

A more amicable relationship? With Rourk Talveston? It was true what people said then: live long enough and you would see everything. In the back of his mind, Mac knew he should consult with the family and with his lawyers before going anywhere near Talveston. But he hadn't gotten where he was by being cautious. Besides, the offer intrigued him. He didn't doubt for a moment that Talveston had something up his sleeve, and he wanted to find out what it was.

"Sure," he said. "I'll have my assistant call your office. How about this weekend?"

"Sounds good to me." With a grin that gave Mac even more to think about, Rourk Talveston bounded down the steps and disappeared into his car.

The phone rang just as Sabrina got out of the shower. She groaned, grabbed a towel and was wrapping it around herself as she padded into the bedroom.

"Hello?"

"Hi, princess. Hope I'm not catching you at a bad time."

Her hand tightened on the receiver. Slowly, she sat down on the edge of the bed and forced herself to take a deep breath. Her voice shook only a little. "Hi, Dad. Any point in asking how you figured out where I was?"

"Now, sweetheart, do we need to get into all that? You know I've got your best interests at heart. It's true I was angry when you said you wanted a place

of your own, but I've thought things over and decided
I was wrong. You're a grown woman. You've got a
right to a life of your own.''

She'd fallen in the shower and banged her head really badly. She was hallucinating. That had to be the
explanation.

"Dad...are you all right?"

He laughed and she had a sudden image of him,
leaning back in the big chair behind his desk, his feet
propped up on the marble surface, flashing a grin that
was second cousin to a shark's.

"I'm fine, how about yourself?"

"Great...uh, just great."

"Doing anything particular?"

"Working..." No, she wasn't going to fall into his
trap. Although she figured that if he knew where she
was living, he probably also knew that she was working at the restaurant, she wasn't about to get into a
discussion about it.

To her surprise, her father didn't seem inclined to
probe further. "Good, good, but I hope you're not
working all the time. You know I made that mistake.
You've got to have some balance in your life."

First, he'd said he was wrong and now he was telling her he'd made a mistake? Sabrina held the receiver
away from her ear and stared at it. The voice on the
other end certainly sounded like her father's. What
could possibly account for such a drastic change in his
attitude?

"Dad...you're sure nothing's wrong?"

"Sweetheart, everything's fine. Oh, sure, I'm feeling a little more tired than usual, but you've got to expect that at my age.''

So far as she knew, Rourk Talveston had never admitted being tired before in his life. She couldn't even imagine him experiencing so intrinsically human a condition. Hesitantly, she asked, ''You're not sick, are you?''

''Who, me? Of course not. If I was sick, I'd go see that damn fool doctor of mine, but then what does he know anyway?''

Now she really was alarmed. Had he been to the doctor and learned something he wasn't telling her? He was certainly behaving oddly. What if he really was ill?

''Dad...you'd tell me, wouldn't you, if you weren't feeling well?''

There was silence for a moment, then he said, ''Now, princess, you know how I feel about worrying you. But I'll tell you what, why don't you come home this weekend? We can smooth everything over and have a nice talk. It's true I do have one or two things on my mind.''

''*This* weekend?'' She thought fast. Jenny was fully recovered, and much as Sylvia had been enjoying a little break, Sabrina didn't think she would mind coming back to work for at least a couple of days. Besides, her father had never sounded like this before. He wasn't a young man anymore, as difficult as his driving will made it for him to realize. Though they had parted in anger, it hadn't changed her love for him. If he needed her, she would be there in a flash.

"Of course, I'll come," she said. "Sooner, if you like."

There was a pause, then Rourk said gently, "No, princess, this weekend will be fine." He was silent again for a moment before adding, "You've always had a gentle heart, Sabrina. Your mother was the same."

A tremor ran through Sabrina. Her father had never spoken to her of her dead mother. Were it not for the Giacannas, she wouldn't have known anything of her. Now, suddenly, her father seemed willing to change that.

"Thank you," she murmured. "I'll be there."

Mac listened to the busy signal, frowned and hung up. He had to get to the work site. Maybe he could catch Sabrina at the restaurant or just try her again later. Either way, he wasn't going to wait long before implementing the decision he'd made. For whatever reasons—and he hadn't cared to examine them too closely—he was going to tell her the truth about himself. The masquerade had gone on long enough. Besides, in all fairness, he couldn't expect her to be honest with him if he wasn't willing to do the same.

So he would tell her the truth, and while he was at it, he would ask her to come with him to Talveston's place for the weekend. Mac grinned at the thought. She was likely to be a little nervous about the idea, and he couldn't really blame her. But he would take it slowly. Maybe they wouldn't even share a bed. They would have time together, though, and they would get to know each other better so that when they got back to New York— He smiled in anticipation.

The smile didn't last long. Work was going well on the site, but there were the usual problems and they demanded his attention through the rest of the day. He barely had a chance even to think of Sabrina, much less talk with her. It was past quitting time when he finally got a moment to himself. He thought of just going over to the restaurant, but he'd gotten showered with mud when a high-pressure hose broke loose. He grinned at the thought of the impression he would make on the clientele.

Instead, reluctantly he picked up the phone in the trailer. Joseph answered, greeted him cordially and put the call through to the kitchen. Sabrina sounded a little rushed but very much in control.

"I know you're busy right now," he said, "I just wanted to know if you're free this weekend."

"This weekend..." Disappointment rippled through her. She was still acutely self-conscious about what had happened between them the previous evening. Her own behavior astounded and to a certain extent dismayed her, yet she couldn't deny that she desperately wanted to see Mac again.

"I'm sorry," she said with real regret, "but I've promised my dad that I'd go home to see him this weekend. I'm not sure, but I'm worried he may be having a problem of some kind."

"I'm sorry to hear that." His regret was true on several fronts. He felt a piercing sadness at not having her with him, odd since he had never thought to mix business with pleasure before. But along with that, he respected her commitment to her family, being the same way himself.

"I'll call you Monday then," he said. They spoke a few minutes longer before hanging up, both with obvious reluctance.

Sabrina took the train to Greenwich just after rush hour. Sylvia had insisted on coming to the restaurant to do dinner, freeing Sabrina to leave early. She'd left her car behind when she moved out of her father's house in the affluent suburban town northeast of the city. Although she missed the convenience of having her own transportation, she didn't see herself coping with New York traffic. Mac, on the other hand, had no problem with it.

A sigh escaped her. She leaned back against the seat and stared out the window. She should be thinking about her father, trying to anticipate what could be wrong and how she could help. Instead, her thoughts kept returning to Mac as though drawn to a homing beacon. She couldn't escape him no matter how she tried.

Perhaps the solution was to stop trying. Much as she dreaded it, she couldn't put off telling him the truth about herself any longer. Hopefully he would understand and not be too angry, or even worse, reject her because of the social gulf between them. If she was very lucky, he might even find it amusing.

The train pulled into Greenwich station. She gathered her belongings and followed the rest of the people getting off. Her father's driver was at the bottom of the terminal steps, waiting for her. He smiled politely, took her bag, then led the way to the long, dark car parked at the curb. Settled in the back seat, Sabrina stiffened as the driver closed the door and walked around to get behind the wheel. She couldn't elude the sudden sense of having returned full circle to the very place she had meant to leave forever. She was once again Rourk Talveston's daughter, protected and cosseted but never allowed more than a glimpse of freedom.

Firmly she pushed the thought aside. She'd come home because she genuinely cared for her father and wanted to have a good relationship with him, this time as an independent, adult woman capable of making her own decisions. He had said he accepted that, and she had to believe it was true.

By the next morning, belief had faded to hope that was threatening to fade fast. Her father had been delighted to see her, welcoming her literally with open arms. He was warm, humorous, outgoing—and utterly evasive. Try though she did, she couldn't get him to give even a hint of why he had wanted to see her. He'd laughed off her concerns and cut the evening short to make business calls.

She'd gone to bed early, slept badly and woke with a headache. Breakfasting alone in the elegant family dining room that looked out over the gardens and beyond to Long Island Sound, she wondered if she hadn't made a mistake. Perhaps she should return to the city. If her father wasn't even going to talk with her, there didn't seem much point being home.

She found him in the exercise room, finishing up a set on the rowing machine. He looked surprised to see her.

"Up already, princess?"

Sabrina grimaced. She had tried for years to convince him to drop that particular nickname with no more success than she had convincing him that she didn't lie about in bed until noon, rising only to do her nails and nibble on bonbons.

"I've been up for a while now, Dad," she said. "I was hoping we could talk."

Rourk Talveston looked at the breathtakingly beautiful young woman before him and felt his throat tighten. Sabrina resembled his dead wife so much that he had never been able to be in her presence without feeling a stab of pain, although he kept that well concealed just as he did every other emotion of any real significance.

He hoped he wasn't making a mistake. Mac Donnelly wasn't like the other men he'd considered for his daughter. He was aggressive, ruthless, tough as nails and in certain circumstances outrightly dangerous. The discovery that Donnelly was dating Sabrina had come as an unwelcome shock. Rourk's first reaction was fury, followed by deep concern and finally bewilderment. Sabrina had made it clear that she had no interest in a marriage to further her father's business interest—in fact, she'd been offended by the very idea. Yet here she was dating Talveston's chief—and only—competitor.

Donnelly's own behavior was odd. According to the detectives assigned to watch Sabrina after she'd insisted on going out on her own, Donnelly dressed like a workman, drove a pickup, didn't take Sabrina to his own apartment and in general acted completely out of character.

The result was that all of Rourk's instincts told him he needed to take control of the situation. If Donnelly had any thought of using Sabrina to get at Rourk, he was going to be stopped cold. On the other hand, the possibility of Donnelly as a son-in-law had a definite appeal. Enough so that Rourk already had his attorneys getting a head start on the prenuptial agreement that no doubt would involve months of intense negotiations.

But he was getting ahead of himself. First, he needed to assess Donnelly's intentions, and the best place to do that was on his own territory, assuming that he could keep Sabrina from bolting.

"Of course. Let's talk, sweetheart," he said. Standing up, he plucked a towel from the nearby rack, dabbed at his face, then looped the towel across the back of his neck.

"Have you had breakfast yet?" Taking her elbow solicitously—and firmly—he guided her back toward the family dining room.

"I've eaten, but I'll keep you company."

"That's great. Just give me a few minutes, all right? I'll grab a quick shower and join you."

Schooling herself to be patient, Sabrina returned to the dining room. She poured another cup of coffee and leafed through the morning papers. Fifteen minutes passed, then another. She stood up, roamed around the room, stared out the windows and checked the clock again. It was now forty-five minutes since her father had left for that ''quick'' shower, and there was still no sign of him.

A flush of healthy anger went through her. Rourk Talveston might be able to brush off the sycophants drawn like moths to his wealth and power, but his daughter was another matter altogether. He'd gotten her to Connecticut to talk, and that was damn well what they were going to do. Otherwise, she was leaving.

Walking back into the center hallway, intent on finding him, she bumped into the housekeeper instead. Mrs. Rosedale was hurrying toward the stairs with a large bouquet of fresh flowers. The two almost collided. Only Sabrina's quick reflexes kept both the older woman and the crystal vase from falling.

''Oh, my, I am sorry,'' the housekeeper exclaimed. ''I'm in such a rush this morning, Miss Sabrina, what with just learning about the guest and all.''

Sabrina righted a tulip, summoned a smile and asked, ''Guest?''

Mrs. Rosedale shook her head ruefully. ''Now don't be telling me Mr. Talveston forgot to tell you, too? Isn't that just like the man. Invites the gentleman for the weekend and doesn't think to mention it to anyone until he's practically on the doorstep.''

"Isn't it just?" Sabrina murmured. A hollow feeling opened in the pit of her stomach. She'd been so certain that this time her father was being honest with her and that he wasn't just trying to manipulate her into doing what he wanted yet again.

She blinked hard as her smile wavered then disappeared altogether. "And who would this gentleman be, Mrs. Rosedale?"

Someone her father had already tried to foist off on her or someone new? Not that it made any difference. They were all the same, suits with avaricious eyes and clammy hands. The thought alone was enough to sicken her.

"A Mr. Dunleavy, miss."

Sabrina didn't know anyone named Dunleavy, and she didn't care to. She would get her things together and be gone before the mystery guest got anywhere near her.

Mrs. Rosedale smiled weakly. "At least, I think that's it. You know how I am with names. You wouldn't happen to know the gentleman, would you? I ask because Mr. Talveston said to put him in the room next to yours, so I thought perhaps you were acquainted. That would be a great help, if you were. I've no idea what his preferences might be — if there's something we shouldn't serve, for instance — and Mr. Talveston did say he wanted the weekend to go smoothly. Not to criticize in any way, miss, but it would be a tremendous help if we could just get a bit more notice. Not that we don't usually. It's actually

very odd for Mr. Talveston to be so forgetful. I'm sure
he just didn't think to mention it—''

"I'm sure he didn't," Sabrina broke in. She was
surprised by how very normal her voice sounded when
everything inside her was in free fall. How incredibly
stupid and naive her father must think her. How ready
he was to mislead and manipulate her, with no regard
to her own feelings, as though she really wasn't a person at all but just a tool to do his bidding.

Pain made her press her lips tightly together. The
realization of just how badly she had misjudged the
only parent she had ever known almost shattered her
composure. Only pride came to her rescue.

"I don't know Mr. Dunleavy," she said. Taking the
vase from Mrs. Rosedale, she walked up the curving
marble stairs. The housekeeper followed along. At the
top of the steps, Sabrina said. "I'll put these in the
guest room. Would you be kind enough to call the car
around for me? I've had a change of plans. I won't be
staying after all."

The older woman nodded but was clearly perplexed.
"Of course, miss, but are you certain? Mr. Talveston
did say there would be three for dinner, so I know
he's expecting—''

"He'll just have to get along without me. The car,
please."

Mrs. Rosedale went off, but not without a worried
glance over her shoulder. Sabrina stepped into the
guest room, sumptuously furnished as was every room
in Rourk Talveston's home. His home, not hers. She
would never again be so foolish as to forget that.

"Have a nice weekend, Mr. Dunleavy," she murmured to the air before quickly returning to her own room. It took only minutes to toss her few belongings into the small bag she'd brought with her, and only a moment longer to take a last, quick look around the room. Her head high and her step firm, Sabrina walked down the stairs and straight out the front door.

The car was already there, the driver holding the door open for her. "The station, please."

"As you wish, miss."

She got into the back seat and stared straight ahead. No matter what, she wasn't going to cry, but the hurt was so great that she had to close her eyes against it.

And therefore did not see the sleek sports car that had been coming up the wide, circular driveway, the car that slowed almost to a stop just as she came out of the house, and stood idling until she had disappeared from view, then slowly continued down the driveway, back through the gates, and away.

Chapter 5

Mac's knuckles were white against the black leather of the steering wheel. Fury almost blinded him. He took a deep breath, fighting for control, but without complete success.

The little witch. She and her father had played him well, setting the hook without him even seeing it for what it was, coming so very close to reeling him in completely that even now he could feel the tug of longing so sharp it made him curse viciously.

What had they imagined? That he would desire Sabrina so much that discovering she was his archrival's daughter would make no difference to him? That all Sabrina's pretended innocence and sweetness would leave him thinking with his glands instead of his brain? That he would be so besotted he would go along with whatever Talveston wanted?

All that and probably more. Worse yet, they'd been right. The savage pain ripping through him told Mac how very close they had come to succeeding.

A harsh laugh broke from him. He'd actually been so far gone as to unknowingly invite her to her own father's house just because he didn't want to be separated from her for a weekend. How she must have laughed over that, savoring the success that was just within reach.

They were two of a kind, Talveston and his beautiful, treacherous daughter. Twenty-five years before, when Rourk Talveston was just starting out, he'd taken advantage of Quinn Donnelly's grief over his wife's death to destroy the company the Donnelly brothers had built with their own sweat and blood. No one had been able to stop him then, but Mac had vowed revenge. He'd created Century Construction and built it step by relentless step at least in part to shatter Talveston's supremacy. Now, with that goal almost in his grasp, he'd only just discovered how very clever his adversary—and his adversary's daughter—really were.

Still, he had to give credit where it was due. Rourk was good, but Sabrina was better. Of course, she had weapons her father couldn't match—ethereal beauty matched with earthy sensuality, all wrapped up in the acting skills of an Oscar winner. The plain fact of the matter was that she'd come within an inch of making a complete fool of him.

And she was going to pay.

A hard, merciless smile curved his mouth as he considered exactly what would be fitting retribution. The

answer was obvious. She had made him want her as
he'd never wanted a woman in his life. Fine, he would
have her...over and over until he was sated with her.
Then he would toss her away. A tiny twinge of guilt
tried to make itself known, but he repressed it firmly.
Miss Sabrina Talveston needed a lesson in humility
she would never forget, and he was exactly the man
to administer it.

He tracked the limousine until it pulled in front of
the Greenwich train station and Sabrina got out. When
the limo moved back into traffic, Mac took the same
spot. He left his car and followed her into the station,
staying well back. She bought a ticket and went up to
the New York–bound platform. A few minutes later,
a train arrived and she got on.

He spared a moment to wonder why she was interrupting her weekend, but quickly decided he didn't
care. He was back in the city within the hour and
hanging up the phone, his plans made, not long after
that. After changing, he headed over to Sabrina's
apartment in the pickup. She had just gotten in, hadn't
even taken off the simple but elegant suede jacket she
wore over silk slacks and a top. Her eyes widened with
surprise when she answered the door to find him standing there.

Mac flashed her a broad smile and stepped into the
apartment before she realized what was happening. "I
thought I'd take a chance and check if maybe your
plans had changed," he said artlessly.

She stared at him, dumbfounded. As always, his
sheer size and overwhelming masculinity disoriented

her. With an effort, she got hold of herself and managed a faint smile. "I thought you were going out of town."

He shrugged his massive shoulders. "I haven't gone yet. Since you're here, want to reconsider and come with me?" Before she could answer, he closed the distance between them. Sabrina was startled to find her back pressed against the wall. Instinctively, she reached out her hands only to have them flattened against his rock-hard chest. He was so near she could feel the warmth of his breath on her cheek. He bent slightly, brushed her mouth with his and murmured, "Come with me, Sabrina."

Her senses whirled. The shock of him being here, the undeniable pleasure and excitement she felt just at seeing him—all combined with the sorrow and anger that still throbbed within her. She wanted to wash away the pain with feelings of an entirely different kind.

And she wanted him. Oh, God help her, how she wanted him.

Unconsciously, she touched the tip of her tongue to lips that suddenly felt dry. "Come where?"

Mac stared at that small, instinctive gesture and for a moment forgot all else except the need to hold and touch her, to make her feel the same surging passion she so effortlessly unleashed in him. Then memory returned and with it yet a further strengthening of his resolve.

She was going to pay.

His smile deepened, a wolfish baring of the teeth as

the gray shards of his eyes glittered like ice floes on an Arctic sea. "My cabin," he said and ran his hand up her arm, observing how she trembled at his touch.

"We'll put the city and everything behind us, and just concentrate on each other."

His voice was low, seductive but reassuringly gentle. His touch was—she had no words for it except that he obviously knew just how and where she was most susceptible. Yet still she hesitated until the memory of the previous evening and all she had felt in his arms swept through her, banishing thought, reason, doubt, *everything* except the overwhelming need to be with him.

"All right," she murmured, her eyes fluttering to his. She was rewarded with a smile that stole the breath from her.

They drove north out of the city, haunting Irish music playing and the windows open to admit the fresh, sweet-scented air. For miles, they followed the course of the river, winding like a silver ribbon beneath rolling hills. The road climbed and the temperature dropped, not unpleasantly but enough to make Sabrina think of sitting in front of a wood fire, Mac close beside her, the two of them hidden away from all the world.

The day had been long and draining, and had come on top of a week of little sleep. Her eyelids were heavy and the soothing rush of motion lulled her even further. A dreamy sigh escaped her as she turned slightly, facing Mac, her head pillowed on her softly folded hands.

He caught himself staring at her and wrenched his gaze back to the road. She looked so damn beautiful, so sweetly innocent that he had to remind himself, for perhaps the dozenth time, that she was nothing at all as she appeared. She was Rourk Talveston's daughter, every bit as deceiving and manipulative as her father, and she deserved exactly what she was going to get.

Besides, it wasn't as though he would hurt her in any way. On the contrary, he was going to bring the lovely Sabrina to a peak of sexual fulfillment unlike any she had ever experienced. Accustomed as she undoubtedly was to using her beauty and sensuality to get what she wanted from men, she was going to discover how readily both could be used against her. He would leave her mindless with pleasure...but he would leave her. Before he was done, she would know beyond any doubt that he was not a man to be controlled by his own desires.

On that grim thought, he let her sleep. After a time, he left the highway for the back roads leading up into the deep forest.

Sabrina woke when the truck went into a particularly deep rut. Jostled from too-brief sleep, she sat up and looked around in some confusion. For a moment, she had no idea where she was or why. When she did remember, she flushed and quickly looked away from Mac. Her own audacity in agreeing to come with him amazed her. She had never done anything so precipitous in her life. Yet she couldn't seem to muster any real regret.

Blinking the last of sleep from her eyes, she stared out at the thick woods. The air was definitely colder. She caught a glimpse of water through the trees, but realized it was a lake rather than the river.

"Where are we?" she murmured.

He told her, but the name meant nothing. She wrapped her jacket more closely around her as she tried to throw off the fog of unaccustomed midday sleep. "Are we almost there?"

He nodded but said nothing more as he maneuvered the truck along the dirt road. The ruts got bad enough that Sabrina grabbed hold of the side of the door and held on tightly. They came around a hard curve and the cabin loomed suddenly in front of them. Sabrina almost sagged with relief, but it was short-lived. Barely had she looked at the building than her eyes widened in disbelief.

It was a cabin—that much, at least, was as she'd expected. There might even have been a time when it was a nice cabin. Nothing extravagant, to be sure, but comfortable enough. Sometime around the last Ice Age, maybe.

Slowly, she got out of the truck and took a deep breath. The air was cold but delicious. Her head cleared rapidly and she allowed herself to believe that perhaps the place wasn't as bad as she'd thought at first glance.

That brief hope fluttered and died as she noticed the porch hanging off the front of the building. One end had collapsed entirely, and there was an alarming sag right in the middle. The door looked sturdy enough, but the windows on either side were encrusted with dirt, the shutters hanging off their hinges.

There was a fireplace, but any thought of curling up in front of it vanished when Mac kicked open the unyielding door and gestured her inside.

"C'mon," he said cheerfully. When she hesitated, he added, "It'll be getting dark soon. Lots of bears around. You don't want to run into them."

Normally she would have agreed wholeheartedly, but as she stood just outside the front door and surveyed the interior of the cabin, she had to consider that the bears might be the better choice. There was one main room haphazardly furnished with pieces she was accustomed to seeing out on a sidewalk. A couch of indeterminate color boasted torn upholstery. A nearby chair was lacking part of one leg and stood upright only with the help of a stack of moldering magazines propped under it. The only table in sight appeared to have been gouged repeatedly with a sharp object, although to be fair the worst scars were hidden by what looked like at least a quarter-inch of accumulated grime.

Out of the corner of her eye she spied a kitchenette, but the mere thought of its likely condition stopped her from looking further. A short flight of steps led up to a loft and what were apparently the sleeping quarters.

"Guess maybe I should have cleaned up a little last time I was here," Mac said. He lifted a stack of old magazines off the couch, then dropped them onto the floor with a resounding thud. "Still, a little mess never hurt anyone, right?"

Sabrina's mouth was hanging open. She shut it firmly, took a deep breath and said, "No, I don't suppose a little mess ever did." Even as she spoke, her mind reeled. He couldn't really believe this was a *little mess,* could he?

On the heels of that thought came a wave of self-consciousness and something very close to shame. Mac worked far harder than she had in her whole life and he didn't have the benefit of a cushy trust fund to fall back on if the need ever arose. He undoubtedly had little time for relaxation, plus he'd grown up in a household of men without the benefit of a woman's touch. If he happened to be somewhat less fastidious about his surroundings than she was, who was she to condemn him for it?

She realized he was watching her. The thought that he might be concerned about her reaction strengthened Sabrina's determination not to let him see how she felt. Brightly, she said, "The setting is lovely."

That much was certainly true. The cabin sat surrounded by deep pine woods on the edge of a crystalline lake. It could be truly idyllic, assuming the blight on the landscape that she was standing in could just vanish.

"Yeah, well…" He stuck his hands in his hip pockets and shrugged those impossibly broad shoulders. "We left in kind of a hurry. I'll take a ride into town and pick up some groceries. You can get settled."

He was out the door before Sabrina realized he truly meant to leave her in a place where she didn't feel very confident about turning around, much less *settling*.

Halfway down the road, Mac felt a twinge of conscience. It really was a dirty trick to abandon her in the old cabin, but if he stayed there much longer, looking at her stricken face, he was going to blow the whole plan. It was all he could do not to sweep her up in his arms, tell her it had been a joke and take her off to the very nice lodge he had less than half a mile away.

The cabin had come with the property and he'd actually used it once or twice while the lodge was being built, but he hadn't been in it in almost a year and it was definitely the worse for wear. A few hours stuck there were guaranteed to take the starch out of Sabrina.

By the time he got back, she would be a wreck. He intended to tell her he'd had second thoughts and arranged to borrow a place nearby. A smile curved his hard mouth as he contemplated the form her gratitude was likely to take.

Sabrina listened to the sound of the truck ebbing away and closed her eyes. She lifted her lids slowly, peering beneath the thick fringe of lashes. Perhaps at second glance the cabin would look more appealing.

It didn't.

Grimacing, she took a deep breath and tried to decide what to do. Mac had left so abruptly that she had a horrible suspicion he was concerned about—perhaps

even embarrassed by—her reaction. She deeply re-
gretted that. If she could have, she would have gone
after him at once and reassured him that everything
was really fine.

Since that wasn't possible, she came to a decision.
She might as well make herself useful and at the same
time make amends for her rudeness. Never mind that
she'd grown up with a houseful of servants; the first
and in some ways the most important lessons any
would-be chef received had far more to do with clean-
ing than cooking. Determined, she began looking
around for what she would need.

Armed with supplies and a bucket of steaming water, she tackled the kitchen first. The dirt that lay everywhere turned out to be dust. It yielded quickly to
her efforts.

Encouraged, she headed for the main room. The
chimney drew her attention. She knelt down and cautiously stuck a piece of kindling up the flue to make
sure it was open. Still hesitant, she lit one end of the
wood and watched the smoke rise unimpeded. Reassured that she wouldn't be in danger of suffocation,
she swept the fireplace out, laid a new fire and soon
had a cheerful blaze to accompany her efforts.

Deciding to investigate the upstairs before proceed-
ing any further, she climbed the steps and found herself in a sleeping loft that was in surprisingly good
condition. A bath was tucked away behind a rough
pine door. Most of the loft was taken up by a king-
size platform bed with a large, hand-carved wooden
chest at its foot.

Before she could think too much about it, she took linens from the chest, and quickly made up the bed. Her cheeks warmed as she finished and stood back for just a moment to contemplate the results. Covered with a striped Hudson's Bay blanket and pillows covered in flannel plaid, the bed looked undeniably inviting. She thought of the serious possibility that she would be sharing it with Mac come nightfall, and bit her lower lip.

She'd known perfectly well what he intended when he asked her to come away with him for the weekend. They had been leading up to this from the first moment they met. Even if everything was happening far faster than she would ever have believed possible, she couldn't find it in herself to feel regret. Nervousness was another matter altogether. Even panic wasn't completely out of the question.

Determined to distract herself, she went back downstairs and tackled the main room. The dust was thicker there and she had to open the windows to keep from coughing, but she made steady progress. Inevitably, though, too many nights without proper sleep took their toll and she began to flag. When she caught herself polishing the same surface over and over, she decided a little rest wouldn't hurt. Resolving to stop for just a few minutes, she settled down in front of the fire.

It was a whole lot harder to stay away than Mac had expected. He stopped at the diner in town and ordered a sandwich, then found he couldn't eat it because he was worrying about when Sabrina had eaten last and whether she was hungry. It didn't get any better at the grocery where he picked up supplies. He killed another hour at the pool hall but he'd been watching the clock the whole time and it was with great relief that he decided he'd been gone long enough. He drove back at a speed he would normally have considered reckless and had to force himself to slow down before taking the final curve to the shack.

Barely had he done so when he smelled smoke. A curse broke from him as he jammed on the brakes, hurled himself from the truck and ran toward the cabin. He was through the door and halfway across the single room when he stopped abruptly.

There was a fire, all right, but it was in the fireplace. And it cast a cheery glow over a scene he could scarcely credit. The piles of debris were gone from the room. The furniture had been straightened, a clean blanket tossed over the couch to hide its condition and the broken chair removed. The table not only gleamed, but was adorned with a bouquet of wildflowers in a tin pot. He dared a quick look in the kitchen and saw the same efforts had been made there. The sink and stove top shone, and the counter and cabinets were startlingly clean. Even the windows sparkled, having apparently been washed.

Disbelief held him frozen for a moment before his gaze fell on the woman lying curled up on the rug in front of the fire. He crossed with rapid strides to stand next to her, then went down on his haunches. His hand was gentle as he brushed the hair back from her face.

"Sabrina..."

She stirred slightly but did not wake. He watched the slow rise and fall of her chest before quietly standing. Again, he looked around the cabin and again he shook his head in bewilderment. He had fully expected to return to find her anger so great it would override even her determination to deceive him. He'd looked forward to confusing her with pretended repentance, then dazzling her with hot, demanding sex.

Instead, he found her asleep, her hands still red and damp from what must have been an exhausting menial effort. It made no sense and it certainly didn't accord with what he knew of her. His eyebrows drew together as he looked down at her sleeping form. Even unconscious, she was the most incredibly beautiful and desirable woman he had ever met. But he had to admit, if only to himself, that she was also far more clever than he would have thought possible. By refusing to act as he'd expected, she'd come very close to undermining his resolve.

Fortunately, close only counted in horseshoes.

Deliberately, he turned his back on her and went into the kitchen. He would give her a little longer to rest—and himself a little longer to shore up his resolve. Grimly, he acknowledged that he needed it. If only she didn't look so damn fragile. If only he didn't have such a nearly overwhelming urge to comfort and protect her. If only she wasn't who she was.

A curse broke from him. He unloaded the supplies he'd bought and started to brew a pot of coffee, then caught himself wondering if Sabrina would prefer tea and cursed again. By dint of sheer effort, he made it through five minutes, but at the end of them he found himself standing over her once again. She was going to get a crick in her neck if she lay like that much longer.

One thing he had to give the woman, she sure could sleep—first in the truck, now here. He had to wonder why she was so tired, and if it could possibly have anything to do with the same reason he'd been sleeping so poorly himself.

Another quarter hour passed before he realized she wasn't going to wake up anytime soon. She gave a small sigh when he lifted her and snuggled against his chest. Mac just barely managed to stifle a groan. He'd known plenty of women who were deliberately, even artfully enticing, but he'd never met one before who could be dead to the world yet still manage to arouse him so intensely that he had to summon all his self-discipline not to wake her then and there.

He stopped at the top of the steps and stared at the bed for a long moment before gently laying her on it. He slipped off her shoes, then eased her under the covers. As he drew the blanket up over her shoulders, he lingered, the back of his hand gently brushing her petal-smooth cheek. She smiled faintly and nestled against him, as though seeking his touch. The gesture was so innocent that it sent a wave of tenderness through him, greatly at odds with the pounding of his heart or the insistent hardening of his body.

Grimacing at his own susceptibility, he left her and went back downstairs. Having taken another long, thorough look at her handiwork, he added wood to the fire, then went into the kitchen.

Sabrina woke some time later from a dream that featured calliope music, dancing clowns with bright red noses, a beautiful lady wearing purple spangles astride a white horse and a hot dog decorated with a squiggle of bright yellow mustard. Her eyes still closed, she tried to hold on to the dream only to have it fade like wisps of fog before the morning sun. The faint whisper of the music remained a little while longer until it, too, was gone. But the hot dog stayed, or at least the scent of it did.

She opened her eyes and sat up slowly. She was in the sleeping loft, on the big bed, covered with a blanket. She vaguely remembered feeling very tired, sitting down in front of the fire. Her cheeks flushed as she realized Mac must have come back, found her and carried her up here.

And now he was…cooking?

Her nose twitched. She hadn't eaten a hot dog in how many years…ten, fifteen? But she had no difficulty recognizing the aroma. To her utter astonishment, her stomach growled.

Still blinking away sleep, she padded down the stairs. Mac was in the kitchen, his back turned to her. She paused for a moment, her attention caught by the broad sweep of his back, tapering to a narrow waist. The jeans he wore did little to conceal the power of his hard, sculpted thighs or the muscular curve of his—

She yanked her eyes away and deliberately pinned on a smile.

"Hi."

His shoulders stiffened for just an instant before he turned. He didn't smile, but his gaze moved over her with a slow thoroughness that stripped away the small amount of self-confidence she'd managed to muster. She was suddenly all too aware of her tangled hair and wrinkled clothes, the redness of her hands. Wincing, she said, "I must be a sight."

Without taking his eyes from her, he said slowly, "Yeah, you are." His voice was deep and slightly roughened. He moved toward her. She had to fight the urge of retreat, to stand her ground. Her chin lifted and unconsciously she straightened her back.

"Quite a sight," he murmured with an odd gentleness that pierced her. He touched a stray curl, wrapped it around his finger and drew her closer. Her lips parted on a soundless sigh. She gazed up at him, uncertain, startled by the rush of feeling he so effortlessly provoked. Without realizing what she did, her tongue touched her lips in a small, nervous gesture.

It was too much for Mac. The days and nights of unfulfilled desire had brought his self-control to the breaking point and forced him to confront the truth, stunning as it was. The beautiful, enchanting deceiver he held in his arms was different from every other woman he had known. He liked the women he had bedded, often admired their work in their own spheres and enjoyed them as individuals, but none had ever affected him as Sabrina did. What he felt for her was savage, ruthless, utterly primitive. He wanted to possess her in every way possible, to both punish her for callously using her body to manipulate him into forgetting his own duty and responsibility and at the same time pleasure her until she was mindless to anything but her need for him. Him as a man, not a balance statement. And, damn it, before this night was over, she would know him as a man so thoroughly that she would never be able to think of him in any other way.

His resolve arrived at, he did not hesitate longer than it took to quickly flick off the stove. Pulling her hard against him, he raked his fingers through her hair to cup the nape of her neck, then fastened his mouth on hers.

It was a kiss unlike any they had shared before, filled with raw, hot demand. He didn't coax or ask, but simply took, parting her lips with his, tasting her deeply, his tongue thrusting with a dark, potent rhythm that made the muscles of her abdomen clench and her knees buckle. Her first reaction was alarm, but barely had the first tendrils of real fear begun within her than they were banished by the sweet upsurge of her own need. She eased her hands up between them, stroking the hard planes of his chest, and was rewarded by the harsh groan wrung from him.

Mac tore his mouth from hers and took hold of her hips, moving her against him as his lips traced a line of fire down the vulnerable silkiness of her throat to the shadowed cleft between her breasts. She gasped and clung to him, her nails digging into his shoulders as the world careened out of control.

Dimly, as though through a throbbing, red mist, Mac realized that he was on the verge of taking her standing up against the kitchen counter. He couldn't do that, not this first time, no matter what she had done. Lifting her swiftly, he strode into the main room. He yanked the blanket off the couch, laid it on the floor in front of the fire and placed Sabrina on it.

In the glow of the flames, she looked like a young goddess, her skin pale as ivory, her hair like the finest spun gold. She opened her eyes to gaze up at him, and he was reminded irresistibly of the softest spring day when the earth stirs with new life. Groaning, he yanked his boots off and came down over her, holding his weight on his forearms.

"You're the most beautiful thing I've ever seen," he said, his voice gruff and hard. His hands slid up under the delicate silk of her blouse, closing around her ribs before moving to cup her breasts. "The first time I set eyes on you, I wasn't even sure you were real." His searching fingers found the front clasp of her bra and swiftly undid it. She gasped as his heat seared her, his calloused palms rubbing over her distended nipples. She moaned helplessly, her hips arching as she instinctively tried to get closer to him. The silver glint of his eyes scorched her. "That's it, sweetheart, tell me what you want."

Sabrina was almost beyond speech, beyond thought, and certainly far beyond reason. Nothing in her life had prepared her for this. Dimly, she sensed she ought to have some reserve or at least hesitation, but she couldn't muster either. Nothing mattered except Mac and the incredible feelings he unleashed within her.

"Tell me," he said again, demanding now. As though to emphasize his command, his big hands moved, stretching the fabric of her blouse until the buttons gave way from the inside. He lifted her easily, stripping away that garment and her bra, leaving her naked to the waist. She had only a moment to draw breath before his mouth closed on her breast, his tongue laving the nipple before drawing it in to suckle her.

Sabrina cried out. Pleasure unlike any she had ever experienced seized her. She tried to clasp him to her but he seized both her hands with one of his, shackling her at the wrists and stretching her arms above her head. For Mac, the action was absolutely necessary. If she touched him, he thought he would go up in flames. As it was, his control was perilously close to snapping.

That wouldn't do. He had no interest in hasty sex. He wanted it slow, drawn-out, wanted her panting and begging.

God, he couldn't keep thinking like that and have any hope of holding on. Raising himself slightly, he undid the waistband of her slacks and eased them down her hips. His eyes flared as he saw how delicately made she was, how lithe and graceful. He brought her arms down, still holding her in place, and began kissing her all over—her face, her throat, her breasts, down to the satiny plane of her stomach and below.

"You taste so sweet," he said hoarsely when he

finally raised his head and stared at the dazed, languorous woman beneath him. Her eyes were heavy-lidded, her mouth full and trembling, a slight flush darkening the lush swell of her breasts to the erect peaks.

"Mac." She whispered his name even as she tried to reach for him, but her limbs felt so heavy, the blood surging through them molten, every nerve ending throbbing. She could only lie still and acquiescent as he removed her few remaining garments, baring her completely to him.

A low groan broke from him when he saw her completely for the first time. She was perfectly formed, elegant but sensual, everything he could ask in a woman. But there was also an ineffable air of innocence that even now, even knowing what he did about her, made him ache with the need to protect her.

That was absurd. If anything, he was the one who needed protection from her unique brand of ingenuous treachery. He had to remember that—*had to*—or he would be lost.

His breathing harsh, his heart pounding, he stripped off his own clothes. So swift was he that he did not notice Sabrina's stunned fascination, the dark dilation of her pupils as she gazed at the hard, rippling muscles that sculpted his shoulders and chest, rippling along his abdomen to steely thighs and—

She looked away hastily but not before alarm pierced the erotic dazzlement of her senses. Instinctively, she began to rise. He stopped her with humiliating ease simply by lowering his body once again over hers.

''Now where were we?'' he said with a smile of such pure male confidence it stole her breath away. As though to answer his own question, his big hands clasped her hips, lifting her to receive the caress of his mouth even as his thigh moved between hers, opening her for him. Sabrina had never felt so acutely vulnerable or so helplessly enthralled. She wanted to protest, but the words wouldn't come. She wanted him to stop, and dreaded that he might. She wanted... whatever it was shimmering off just beyond her reach, the heavy, tremulous tightening within her, the steadily building tension that was leading her on and on to some unfathomable pleasure.

Throbbing tremors of sensation coiled tighter and tighter until abruptly they released, piercing her with ecstasy so profound that she screamed. She clung to the man who loomed above her, his face hard with passion, cleaving to his strength as the world dissolved and oblivion took her.

Slowly, so slowly, she became aware of several things—her heart was pounding, her breath came in gasps, and Mac...Mac was waiting, his eyes shards of molten silver. She felt his steely strength against her and gasped even as he began to move. Incredibly, seemingly impossibly, the coils of pleasure began to tighten within her once more, driving her right back into the ecstasy she thought she could not possibly bear so soon.

"I can't," she moaned, her head twisting back and forth on the blanket. *"I can't."*

But in the next instant, she knew better as his hand slipped between her thighs, stroking her, and he bent closer, his breath warm against her cheek, his voice low and dark, sending tremors through her as he whispered what he would do, how he would make her feel.

She was beyond any thought of resistance, beyond even the shred of a doubt, when he moved at last to enter her. The first touch of him made her gasp but she reached out, her arms clutching his broad shoulders, drawing him closer still.

He made a low, guttural sound deep in his throat and surged forward. Sabrina cried out, sobbing his name even as she felt Mac stiffen above her. In the next moment, a rush of cool air touched her heated skin as he raised himself and gazed down at her in disbelief.

"What the hell—?"

Chapter 6

The words just barely penetrated the sensual haze engulfing Sabrina, and even then several moments passed before she realized that Mac was holding himself very still above and in her. The look on his face was changing from incredulity to anger. Terrible, piercing anger.

All the tender passion of her generous nature rebelled against that. No matter what the cost, she would not relinquish the beauty of what they shared. Obeying instincts she had not imagined herself to possess, she clasped his taut hips even as she arched against him, drawing him deeper into her.

A curse broke from him. He cupped her face between his big hands and demanded, "What the hell are you doing? Don't you realize—"

But she did, realized fully and completely that she

could not bear to have him leave her, not like this. If they parted now in anger, there might never be another chance for them.

Besides, she couldn't quite see why he would be angry except that she hadn't been completely honest with him—all right, not at all honest, not about her identity or her experience.

No wonder the man's face was darkening perceptibly, his eyes gleaming dangerously, the hard line of his mouth suggesting he was about to yield to the rage building within him.

Desperately determined that he should yield to her instead, Sabrina reached out to him. She stroked her hands over his powerful chest, down his flat abdomen to where their bodies joined. Touching him as she was sent incredibly powerful sensations trembling through her. Her eyes were wide and luminous, her lips softly parted as she gazed up at him. "Please…Mac…don't stop—"

It was more than he could bear. Hell, no man alive could resist such devastatingly innocent yet utterly feminine entreaty. A groan broke from him as her mouth touched his flat, male nipple, her tongue caressing him with shy yet shattering effectiveness.

"Sabrina…"

The tenuous hold he'd just barely managed to maintain on himself snapped. With a harsh groan, he thrust into her, the rhythm of his hard, deep strokes making Sabrina cry out as she arched beneath him.

"Please…" She sobbed, unaware of her nails raking down his back. *"Please…"*

He slid his hands under her buttocks, lifting her legs over his shoulders so that she was completely open and vulnerable to him. He rode her hard, holding nothing back, demanding everything until the spasms of her release seized them both. So intense was it that Sabrina screamed his name as the world exploded. Mac gave a low, guttural groan and followed her, his big, hard body shuddering with the hammer blows of his own release.

In the aftermath, Mac raised his head slowly, realizing that he was sprawled on top of Sabrina, his breath still labored, his heart pounding furiously. Her arms were around him. She was holding him close. With an effort, he lifted himself from her, and gazed down into her shining eyes.

His knuckles brushed her cheek as he studied her closely. "You should have told me."

"I should have," she agreed, though she hardly looked repentant. The smile that curved her luscious mouth was so female—and so triumphant—that a fresh wave of disgruntlement moved through him. "You wouldn't really have stopped, would you?" she asked, brushing back a lock of ebony hair that had fallen across his forehead.

"I couldn't," Mac said bluntly. "You had me so hot I probably wouldn't have stopped if the whole place was going up in flames."

Her smile deepened even as a startling flush rosed her cheeks. Lowering her gaze, she gave a small sigh and snuggled against him as though it was the most natural thing in the world for them to be lying on the floor like this, her head resting on his bare chest, her silken soft hair tickling him lightly, her satiny limbs entwined with his, the scent of sex clinging to them both. He hesitated but only for a moment before his arms closed around her, cradling her with fierce gentleness.

He'd been stalked, lured, trapped and now trussed with dazzling skill and he knew it. Hell, the side of his nature that made him such an effective business-man couldn't help but admire her strategy. Not only that, but he had to draw some consolation from the fact that she'd had weapons in her arsenal he hadn't even imagined.

Caressing her back with a lazy, circular motion, he said, ''Would you mind telling me something?''

Her lips moved against his chest. ''What?''

''How is it that a woman who looks the way you do could get to be twenty-five years old and still be a virgin?''

She didn't answer at once, and he had begun to think she wouldn't, when finally she said, ''After my mother's death, my father kept me very close. He was obsessed with my safety, understandably enough. I was taught at home until I was fourteen and even then I almost never went anywhere alone.''

''What about more recently?''

''As I got older, I had friends who had been through some experiences they would rather have done with-out. Despite being intelligent women, well educated, successful in their fields, it seemed as though too many of them ended up just feeling used. I'm sure it works both ways,'' she added hastily. ''I'm not putting all the blame on men, but I decided that I'd rather wait.''

''Wait for what?'' he asked, really just to see if she would be at all honest.

Sabrina raised herself up so that she could look at him. The expression in her beautiful eyes made his chest ache even as he told himself he would have to be the world's worst fool to believe it.

''For the right man,'' she said quietly, followed with a becoming blush.

So well-done was it that he flinched only slightly as the final tug on the line set the hook firmly in place.

Sabrina frowned. She wished she could tell what he was thinking, but his expression was unfathomable. He was gentle enough—now—but the enormity of what she had done was beginning to sink in, and it left her deeply shaken. She had shared the ultimate intimacy with a man who didn't even know who she really was because she had deliberately and repeatedly misled him as to her identity. He would have every right to be furiously angry, perhaps even reject her completely. The mere thought made her stomach knot, but she knew what had to be done. Waiting any longer wouldn't make it any easier.

''Mac,'' she said softly, not quite looking at him, ''I have to tell you something....''

He had felt the gathering tension in her before she spoke. That and the sudden anguished uncertainty in her eyes told Mac all he needed to know. He made a lightning decision and rolled over, pinning her beneath him. Before she could speak, he brought his mouth

down hard on hers. "Later," he murmured, his lips
moving against hers. "Tell me later."

Sabrina tried to insist but the sudden, shocking re-
newal of passion stopped her. Her body, already
schooled to his touch, responded instantly. As his
powerful hands stroked her with devastating skill, she
could only moan helplessly and reach out to him.

Some time afterward, Sabrina felt herself being
lifted and carried. She didn't open her eyes, but merely
nestled closer against the hard, warm chest beneath her
cheek. She felt the deep rumble of Mac's chuckle and
smiled.

"Wake up, sweetheart," he said softly as he set her
down, "or this is going to come as an awful shock."

Her eyes opened then and she gazed up at the face
of the man who had taken her to unimagined heights
of ecstasy over and over, giving of himself so generously that she was at once exalted and humbled. The
hard, clean line of his jaw was darkened by a night's
growth of whiskers, reminding her suddenly of the
slight abrasive sensation as he'd kissed her breasts, her
belly, between her thighs. She trembled and gripped
his arm instinctively, steadying herself.

They were in the small bathroom next to the sleeping loft. Mac flicked the shower on, waited while the
water warmed, then lifted her again and gently placed
her in the stall. He followed immediately. Sabrina
gasped as her highly sensitized nipples came into contact with the silky hairs on his chest. Mac made a

harsh sound deep in his throat and moved her the few inches away from him that the tight fit allowed.

"My self-control doesn't extend very far where you're concerned." The corners of his mouth lifted in an expression of chagrin so sharply at odds with his heavy-lidded air of contentment that Sabrina couldn't help but laugh.

His gaze flared like the summer sky when a heat storm was lurking just over the horizon. "That amuses you, does it? We'll see."

He picked up a bar of soap, ran it between his hands, then began to wash her. He started very carefully with her face, tracing her forehead, her cheeks, the straight line of her nose and the curve of her chin, pausing to rinse away the suds before going on down her throat and over her slender shoulders. By the time he had washed each arm down to each separate finger, Sabrina was trembling.

"You don't have to do this," she murmured. "I don't think—"

She stopped on the verge of saying that she couldn't bear it, held by his gaze as he slowly soaped his hands again, then applied them directly to her breasts. As his calloused thumbs rubbed over her nipples, Sabrina's knees gave way. He caught her around the waist, leaning her back against the wall of the shower. Deliberately, methodically, he went on, washing every inch of her, being especially careful and gentle as his hand stroked between her legs where she felt undeniably tender.

Long before he was done, she was so intensely

aroused that she knew it would take very little to send
her over the brink. Mac seemed to know it, too, judg-
ing by the very male smile he gave as he handed her
the soap. "My turn."

Sabrina honestly didn't think she would be able to
do it. She was dazed by the newness and power of her
own feelings, and so sexually stimulated that she
ached. Yet she could hardly deny him the service he
had so generously given her. Taking a deep breath,
she complied. Mac's hands clenched at his sides as
she reached the bulging muscles of his arms. A pulse
leaped to life in his jaw as she lingered over the broad
sweep of his chest. When her hands slipped lower, he
gave a deep, ragged growl and seized them in his own.

"That's enough." He turned the shower off, handed
her a towel and quickly took one for himself. Sabrina
had barely begun to dry herself when he tossed the
towel aside, lifted her and carried her into the bedroom.

"You know," she said a little breathlessly, "I actually can walk."

"Hmm," he murmured, apparently not impressed.
Laying her on the bed, he stepped back and looked at
her.

A wave of embarrassment washed through Sabrina,
but she resisted the impulse to cover herself. Watching
him watching her had an incredibly potent effect. She
felt the touch of his eyes every bit as much as she did
his mouth or hands. A long, sweet quiver of pure need
tightened her body. Her thighs parted even as her hips
instinctively lifted in unmistakable invitation.

Whatever shame she might have felt at such uninhibited behavior melted before the realization of the effect she had on him. His magnificent body was taut with need; his eyes narrowed to glittering shards. As she watched in helpless fascination, he drew a ragged breath and put a knee on the bed beside her.

"I can't get enough of you," he said in a grudging admission that seemed to bewilder him. One big hand cupped her breast as the other stroked her from ankle to hip. "You're a fire in me that won't be quenched."

"Then feed it instead," she whispered and opened her arms to him.

Mac woke from slumber so deep he had no immediate awareness of his surroundings. For several moments, he lay on his back, struggling to full consciousness until he realized that Sabrina was snuggled against him, her head below his shoulder and one slender arm thrown over his chest. She was breathing slowly and steadily in what must have been complete exhaustion.

As he should have been himself, given the incredible excesses of the night, yet something had jerked him into wakefulness. He lifted his head, looked around, but could see nothing amiss in the sleeping loft. Still, sleep would not return and a moment later he knew why. Far in the distance he heard an approaching vehicle.

An instant later, Mac was out of the bed and pulling on his clothes in the main room. He was tucking the shirt into his pants when the early-morning visitor rounded the last curve and came within sight. Mac took one look at the long, black limousine and cursed, but his anger didn't last. It was swiftly replaced by the shrewd intelligence that made him such a formidable competitor and executive.

He had the cabin door open and was lounging against it, his eyes coldly cynical, when Rourk Talveston bolted out of the car and came charging right at him.

"You bastard!" Talveston roared. He didn't pause, but came straight up the rickety porch, his face beet red and his big hands clenched. "I'm going to take you apart, Donnelly. You'll curse the day you ever laid eyes on my daughter. I swear—"

He didn't bother to continue, but instead took a hard, fast swing at Mac. The man might be in his late fifties but he was in damn good shape, and he was fueled by what looked like pure rage. Mac only just managed to duck in time. The chauffeur had gotten out of the car and stood staring in blank amazement as his employer gave every indication of being intent on a knock-down fight to the finish.

Mac had other ideas. He raised both hands, palms out, and took several steps back. "Easy, Talveston, there's no reason for this."

"No reason! Just how stupid do you think I am? You practically kidnap my daughter, bring her to this hovel, and you think I'm just going to—"

"I didn't kidnap her," Mac protested. "Practically or otherwise." He couldn't help smiling as he added,

"And if you think this place is a hovel now, you ought to have seen it before Sabrina went to work on it."

That confused Rourk just long enough to make him hesitate. Mac took quick advantage of it. "We're both reasonable men. We can work this out."

Rourk's gaze narrowed as he stared at Mac. "Whaddya mean work it out? You think I'm gonna stand by and let you use my daughter to get at me?"

"No, I don't." Never mind the thoughts of revenge he'd had the previous day. They didn't count now. "But what if I did? Are you going to try to tell me you weren't planning to use her to get to me?"

The older man's face darkened even further, but he didn't try to deny it. "What if I was? We've been making life tough for each other for too long. It makes a hell of a lot more sense for us to cooperate."

Anger flared in Mac. Up until that moment, he'd held on to some faint possibility that it was all a misunderstanding. Now he knew otherwise. "Maybe you've forgotten what happened twenty-five years ago," he snarled, "but I haven't. So just what the hell makes you think I'd ever cooperate with you?"

Rourk stared at him. He started to speak, stopped and began again. "If I'd known what your father was going through, I would have backed off. All I knew was that he wasn't taking care of business, and he left the way wide-open for me." Head up, challenging, he added, "You would have done the same."

Mac didn't give any credence to Rourk's claim of ignorance. The man was a ruthless, wily manipulator who had never hesitated to use an advantage—any advantage—against an opponent. Mac simply assumed this was one more lie and went right past it.

"What's your excuse for trying to take my company over, or did you just expect the Donnellys to be easy prey a second time?"

"I don't need an excuse," Rourk snapped. "You were in my way. It's only natural I wanted to get rid of you. But you're too tough, too strong and too smart. Hell," he said on a note of disgust, "it got to the point where I actually started to like you."

Again, Mac let that go right past. He simply didn't believe anything Rourk said. Still, he was curious how far he would try to go. "Is that when you cooked up this idea with Sabrina?"

"Now wait a minute, Sabrina didn't—"

"*Dad?*"

Both men turned at that very feminine—and very horrified—exclamation. Sabrina stood framed by the open door, a sheet wrapped around her in a quickly fashioned toga. Her eyes were wide with disbelief and her cheeks were scarlet. As though that weren't enough, her slightly swollen lips and sated glow testified to a largely sleepless night.

"What are you...how...I don't...?" She stopped trying to talk and just stared from one to the other.

Mac was so busy looking at her that he didn't even see Rourk's punch before it slammed into his jaw, but he saw the next one and managed to block it. The outraged-father routine had gotten old fast. "That's enough, Talveston!" He pinned the older man with a wrestling hold around his chest, intending to render him harmless until he could calm down, but the fury of an offended father redoubled Rourk's strength.

"Damn it, Donnelly, there's not gonna be anything left of you when I'm done!"

He broke Mac's grip, sending the two of them tumbling off the porch and into the dirt where they rolled around, Rourk throwing punches, some of which actually connected, until a deluge of icy water showered down on them.

Mac came up first, sputtering, and wiped a forearm across his eyes to clear them. He found himself staring at a white-faced Sabrina still holding the bucket she'd emptied over them. Rourk sat up a little more slowly, eyeing his daughter with caution that under the circumstances was merely prudent.

She looked like a glorious—if pale—virago, Mac thought and couldn't repress his admiration. He got to his feet and started walking toward her.

"Sabrina—"

The deep, piercing anguish in her eyes stopped him cold. He had no idea what to make of it.

"You know each other," she said, her voice unnaturally flat and quiet. A little more loudly, she repeated, "You *know* each other."

Rourk had gotten to his feet. He glanced from Sabrina to Mac and back again. "Of course we know each other. C'mon, honey, how could I not know the guy who's been my toughest competitor for years?"

She was shaking her head dazedly and, if possible, was even more pale than before. "This can't be. He's a foreman…he—"

"He's head of Century Construction. You've heard me mention them."

"Not often...not enough...you never said—" Her voice choked. On a whisper, she said, "You never mentioned anyone by name."

Rourk shrugged, but he had the grace to look abashed. "It's a tough business, I didn't want you bothered. Anyway, let's not get distracted here." He shot Mac a hard look. "Somehow or other the two of you met. How was that exactly, Donnelly? Maybe you can enlighten me as to how that happened?"

"I thought I knew," Mac said slowly. He had not taken his eyes from Sabrina. For the first time since Rourk's arrival, uncertainty stirred in him. Her surprise and distress seemed completely genuine. He'd thought once before that she was putting on an act only to discover it wasn't true. That was a mistake he didn't want to make again. Yet the alternative was to believe that she really was innocent in all ways, that she'd had nothing to do with her father's plotting.

"I assumed you'd gone after her deliberately," Rourk said, filling in the silence. "When my detectives told me that she was—"

"Your detectives?" Sabrina looked at her father with stunned incredulity. "You had detectives following me?"

"I had to! You'd insisted on leaving. I had to make sure you were safe."

"Did it ever occur to you that as a grown woman I'm responsible for my own safety?"

"Did it ever occur to you," Rourk countered, "that

as my daughter, you were more vulnerable than you would have been otherwise? There are kidnappers and…''

Sabrina closed her eyes tightly. When she opened them again, her gaze was filled with understanding and compassion. She went to her father and touched his face gently. ''Dad, I'm so sorry about what happened to Mother. It was a terrible loss for us both, but I don't believe for a moment that she would have wanted us to live in fear because of it.''

His expression softened, but he still wasn't backing down. ''There's a difference between living in fear and taking sensible precautions.''

Watching them both, Mac was struck for the first time by the resemblance between father and daughter. Physically they looked nothing at all alike except for their eyes, but they shared the same steely pride and determination. He wondered that Rourk didn't seem to be aware of that. Could that possibly be?

''I don't think most people would believe that having your daughter tailed by detectives was just sensible,'' Sabrina said. ''It was an invasion of my privacy and it was wrong.'' She glanced at the car and added, ''So was coming here. You have to leave.''

Mac very much doubted that anyone had ever spoken to Rourk Talveston like that before, or at least not in very many years. The man looked positively flummoxed, so much so that Mac actually felt a twinge of sympathy for him.

Just a twinge, though, because his top priority by far was getting Sabrina alone again. They had some serious straightening out to do without any further interference from her father.

"She's right," he said and gestured toward the car. Looking the other man right in the eye, he added quietly, "This is between Sabrina and me."

Rourk stared back at him with a steely glint that suggested he was mentally peeling away the layers of Mac's hide. His mouth thinned. Harshly, he said, "She'd damn well better not be hurt."

For a moment longer, Rourk looked at his daughter. He seemed to want to say something to her, or even reach out and embrace her, but he did neither. With a curt nod, he turned and reentered the car.

The sound of its labored progress down the rutted road faded slowly.

Chapter 7

Sabrina continued to watch the road even after her father's car was no longer in sight. She needed the time to calm herself before she faced Mac. When she did, finally, it was to find him watching her with a caution so great it was almost comical. Or at least it would have been if she hadn't hurt so very badly.

She shivered and pulled the sheet more tightly around herself, aware suddenly of how little protection it offered. Her bare feet peered out from underneath, the toes wiggling slightly in the soft ground covered by pine needles. "I'm not sure we have anything to say to each other."

He sighed and rammed his hands in the pockets of his low-slung jeans. The possibility—he wasn't ready to call it a certainty—that Sabrina hadn't been a part of her father's machinations stunned him. Added to

what he had learned about her in bed, he was forced
to reconsider everything he thought he'd known of her
when he brought her to the cabin. He also had to deal
with an inescapable truth—whatever she'd known or
hadn't known, done or hadn't done, he wanted Sabrina
Giacanna *Talveston* with an intensity that surpassed
anything he had ever experienced. And what Mac
Donnelly wanted, Mac Donnelly got.

"It was you, wasn't it?" she said suddenly, her
voice so faint as to be almost inaudible.

"Wasn't what?"

"Dunleavy. At least that's what Mrs. Rosedale
thought your name was—the unexpected guest my father invited for the weekend."

"Yes," Mac said slowly. "That was me."

"And you invited me to go with you. Was that supposed to be a joke? Were both of you going to surprise
me with your plans?"

He took a step toward her, stopping when she held
up a hand. "I had no idea that you were Rourk Talveston's daughter. You hadn't told me, and I didn't
know it from any other source."

She looked as though she wanted to believe him,
but was very far from sure. "You didn't tell me who
you were either." He noticed she didn't say that she
hadn't known who he was. Sure, she'd said that in the
back-and-forth with her father, but he wanted her to
say it to him, *needed her to say it,* and she didn't.

"Can we call it even?" He spoke as lightly as he
could, but the question was serious. If she was inno-

cent—or even if she wasn't—they had to get past this before they could get anywhere else.

Her eyes looked huge in a too-pale face. Still trying to come to terms with the fact that she was his worst enemy's daughter—and the most incredibly sensual, giving woman he had ever known—he fought the urge to go to her, sweep her up in his arms and make her forget everything except him. Instead, when she didn't answer quickly enough to suit him, he said, "Let's be sensible about this."

Maybe it wasn't the best choice of words. Worse yet, he seemed to be propelled along by some basic male dumbness that was operating like a runaway horse, with him the guy in the saddle trying to yank in the reins even as they slipped between his fingers.

"What I meant was that we both misled each other. That's clear now and we ought to move on."

Sabrina tilted her chin a notch higher, gave him a look that would have frozen lava and said, "That sounds fine to me. The moment I'm dressed, I'm *moving on* as far away from you as I can get."

Anger flared in Mac and underneath it something he didn't want to acknowledge, something that felt an awful lot like fear. He couldn't lose her. Without questioning why that was—mainly because he wasn't ready to deal with the obvious answer—he took hold of her by the shoulders and yanked her against him.

"You're not going anywhere, at least not without me, and you are going to be sensible about this." Desperately, driven by emotions that made it impossible for him even to try playing fair, he said, "In case you didn't happen to notice last night, I was too far out of control to even think about using protection.''

For the first time ever, he had been with a woman without giving a second thought to the consequences. The incredible irresponsibility of that stunned him, all the more so because he couldn't find it in himself to regret it even the least bit.

Sabrina stared at him in dawning realization, then blushed profusely. Dropping her eyes, she said, ''That was both our fault, not just yours.''

The honesty of her response took him aback. He became aware of several things simultaneously—that he was holding her too tightly, that her skin was chilled, and that he was suddenly, almost painfully hard.

He made a low sound deep in his chest and scooped her up, striding back into the cabin. It was a grand gesture, masterful, noble, literally sweeping her off her feet like that, guaranteed to gain him at least a little time before any general reckoning between them. And he knew exactly how he intended to use that time.

Except fate intervened in the form of the decrepit porch. His foot went straight through a plank and he was left, still holding her, with what must have been an at least faintly ridiculous look on his face as he listed noticeably to the side, one leg now significantly shorter than its dangling, trapped match.

''Hmm,'' Sabrina said, looking down at the problem, and laughing.

Something hot and strong unfolded in Mac's chest, a swelling of feeling so all-encompassing that for a moment he truly could not breathe. When he did, it was a gasp hidden beneath a cautious smile. He was suddenly feeling so damn good—still hard, still unsure of so much—because she was laughing, which had to mean she was happy, at least sort of.

He was rambling.

It had just taken him a minute to remember the word for it, because he never, ever did any such thing. At least not in the world Before Sabrina.

"I'm stuck," he said rather unnecessarily and she laughed harder, making them both shake with the force of it.

But her eyes were seriously tender when she looked right into his. "I think that goes for us both."

The woman had a way with words.

This was madness. Plain and simple, classic madness. Nobody got married in this day and age because she'd slept with a guy and *might* be pregnant. Nobody. And that included Sabrina Giacanna Talveston who, even as she stood in the bedroom that had always been hers in her father's Greenwich house and stared at herself in the eighteenth-century full-length mirror in the gilded frame, knew the real reason why she was wearing that exquisitely lovely white silk and lace gown and why she was about to get into a limousine, drive to a church and take vows that would bind her heart and soul to one Mac Donnelly.

She was in love with him.

Which didn't make it one little bit less mad.

But it did make her smile, if somewhat sadly.

She'd lived such a safe life, swathed in the cocoon of her father's fears and determination, that she'd never thought of herself as a risk-taker, yet here she was, leaping out into space, hoping against hope that she would find out she had wings.

That they both did.

Mac didn't love her. She looked at herself in the mirror—eye-to-eye—and made herself repeat the words very clearly in her mind so there was no mistake between the Sabrina she was inside and that outward manifestation that looked so incredibly, foolishly cool and calm.

Mac didn't love her.

He wanted her. It didn't matter that she'd been a virgin a scant week ago, or that he hadn't touched her since that night at the cabin. She knew to the very marrow of her bones that the man wanted her and, further, that he wasn't especially happy about it. He was used to being in control. Everything he was—his work, his life, his very sense of himself as a man— was based on it. She threatened that, so he had to turn the tables, find some way to get control of her.

And of her father's company? A shadow moved behind her eyes. She didn't even want to think of that. Mac wanting her, even without love, she could deal with. It was a beginning at least, something to hold to, maybe even to build on. But a cold-blooded business arrangement was another matter entirely. Against that she would feel powerless.

Up until last night and the hastily thrown-together rehearsal dinner—fitting enough for the hastily thrown-together wedding—her father had still been going on and on about the need for a prenuptial agreement, so much so that Sabrina, loving daughter though she was, had to stifle the impulse to upend one of the many magnums of champagne on the table right over her father's stubborn head.

What stopped her was the suspicion that it was all too superficial to be real and that Mac himself was too calm, sitting back in his chair, enjoying an after-dinner cigar with the other men and several of the women, eyeing Rourk with bland patience through the swirl of smoke.

The gentleman doth protest too much.

Her father was unbearably pleased and struggling with all his might to hide it. Mac was—what? Watchful, calculating, distant? He treated her with cool politeness, which she supposed was better than cool disdain. And why on earth had she suddenly thought of that?

He hadn't touched her in a week, not unless she counted those chaste little pecks on the cheek, which she most certainly did not, or the careful way he held her when they danced, as though they were strangers who were never going to see each other again.

What if she was wrong? What if he didn't want her? What if he'd satisfied his male curiosity about her and was back on track, focused on business the same way he must have been to build such a company in so relatively short a time?

She'd taken pains to learn as much about Century Construction as she could in between the frantic wedding preparations. She'd gone down to the library, found annual reports, scanned the microfilm for every possible story, logged onto the Internet, spent hours and hours reading until her eyes blurred. She'd concluded that she'd been an idiot not to know who Mac Donnelly was.

Except she had been living in Europe and going to school and starting a career and doing all those other things, but even so, she should have known.

Did he think she had?

The eyes in the mirror darkened further. She caught the cool, calm Sabrina chewing on her bottom lip and sighed. It didn't matter what Mac thought, not just then anyway, for the bedroom door was opening, laughter and voices were spilling in. The few precious moments she had stolen for herself were over. It was time.

Mac cursed the tailor who had made the shirt collar too tight, even if it hadn't felt that way up until about half an hour before. He glanced for the hundredth time at the clock in the small room with the walls that seemed to be closing in around him. "It's time."

Quinn gave a broad grin. "You sound anxious, son."

Mac scowled, remembered this was his father he was talking to—and his best man—and sighed. "I just want to get this over with." He yanked the door open and went out into the hallway.

"Aye, sure, that's all there is to it." Quinn laughed and followed.

The church was filled, every seat taken. Despite the short notice, five-hundred-plus guests had cleared their calendars and turned out for the event. Mac scanned them with a cynical eye. Almost without exception, they were business and political associates of Rourk and himself. Only a handful represented family members and friends.

Outside, kept at bay by a cordon of security guards, the media clustered. He wondered if Sabrina had any notion that their wedding was likely to lead the evening news, society and business reporters vying to describe it. He hoped she didn't. Rourk said she'd been too damn busy to notice much of anything, and he wanted that to be true. A hard smile curved his mouth as he reflected that at least she wouldn't be watching television tonight.

The organ swelled, interrupting his thoughts. A hush settled over the guests. One by one, the bride's attendants started down the aisle, arrayed in the colors of high summer like so many gorgeous butterflies, each escorted by a Donnelly brother. Sabrina watched them go from the back of the church. She had a firm hold on her father's arm, but even so the floor seemed to have developed an alarming tilt. Rourk patted her hand reassuringly. She managed a weak smile but it faded as she gazed down the length of the church to the altar and the man awaiting her there.

He looked so breathtakingly handsome, so compellingly masculine—and so undeniably grim. There was nothing remotely soft or tender about him. Dressed in formal black, unrelieved except for the white flash of his shirt, he looked hard as the steel that was the bone and sinew of his buildings.

A flash of panic roared through Sabrina. She was making a terrible mistake, marrying a man she knew didn't love her, a man she herself barely knew. She must have been in the grip of some sort of delusion to even consider it. Perhaps when they had time to get to know each other better, when their feelings deepened—especially his—then it might be reasonable for them to contemplate, slowly and carefully, taking such a step. But not now, not so suddenly and impulsively.

The music paused for just a moment, then resumed on a stately note. Rourk straightened his shoulders, settled his hand over Sabrina's and started down the aisle. Short of digging in her heels and making an awful scene, there was nothing else to do but go along. But since she'd realized she couldn't marry Mac, she would have to make a scene anyway. Was it better to make it at the far end of the aisle or actually wait until she got down to the altar? Maybe she could just whisper something to the minister. Maybe they even had a procedure for dealing with this sort of problem. Who knew, maybe it happened far more often than people realized. It was the kind of thing that would be hushed up. Maybe it was why there were back doors to churches.

"Who gives this woman?"

"I do," Rourk said. His voice was husky. Sabrina looked up and saw tears glistening in his eyes. He leaned a little closer and said softly, "I'm very proud of you, princess."

Then he was stepping back as Mac moved forward

to take her hand and draw her to him. He didn't look grim anymore, just terribly serious, and suddenly, for no sensible reason whatsoever, it was all right. The tightness in Sabrina's throat released, the tingling little bursts of panic disappeared, and she was utterly calm. Never mind that it felt like the calm in the eye of a storm.

Utterly calm and incredibly beautiful. It was all Mac could do to take his eyes from her and face the minister. He felt as though he'd been poleaxed. The rush of feeling that tore through him the moment he saw his bride coming to him, a vision of grace and loveliness drawn from his most deeply held dreams, made him want to throw back his head and roar with triumph. Or just sweep her up in his arms and never let her go. He was filled with elation, near to trembling with it, and that in turn shocked him more than anything else.

He could not—would not—let Sabrina affect him like this. Emotion was danger. Emotion hurt. He'd learned that all too easily when his mother died. And caring about someone too much, especially a woman, could destroy a man. Hadn't his own father nearly suffered that fate, and wasn't Quinn still not the man he would have been if love hadn't so weakened him?

No, he had to be strong and self-contained. Too many people counted on him—his family, his employees—for him to afford the luxury of emotional indulgence. He would be a good husband to Sabrina. He would treat her kindly, keep her in the style to which she was already well accustomed, but he would make damn sure not to let her get too close.

Whatever doubt he felt in his own mind about the feasibility of such a plan was carefully masked, even from himself. Mac spoke his vows in a calm, assured voice. By contrast, Sabrina faltered slightly and he could have sworn her hand shook as he slid the ring on. They turned to face the combined force of a thousand avidly staring eyes and then he really did feel her tremble.

Lowering his head, he whispered, "It will be over soon, sweetheart, just hang on."

She gave him a quick, startled look and managed to smile. Arm in arm, Mr. and Mrs. Mac Donnelly walked down the aisle.

The hours that followed had a dazed, unreal quality to Sabrina. She felt at once a participant and an observer, as though she was both in herself and somehow hovering just outside. She danced with Mac, her father, Quinn and each of her new brothers-in-law, then with a bevy of Giacannas, Joseph leading the way while Sylvia danced with Mac, not hiding her delight at being matron of honor. Sylvia's daughter, Jenny, who had been the flower girl, joined them, making them both laugh as she plucked a few leftover petals from her pockets and dribbled them over the dance floor.

Sabrina chatted with the guests, accepting their congratulations and deflecting their questions—some subtle, some frank—about so speedy a wedding. She posed for photographs, sipped champagne, moved food around on her plate and made every effort to look as though she was having a wonderful time.

She was scared to death. That brief moment of blissful calm hadn't even lasted through the exchange of vows. All the doubts that assailed her earlier were back with a vengeance. Only those few whispered words from Mac kept her from being absolutely certain that she had made the worst mistake of her life.

He didn't love her, but he did seem to care—at least a little. Like it or not, fair or not, there was something about the man that made her feel absurdly safe and secure, absurdly because she knew there was no real reason to feel as she did, not to mention that she was determined to stand on her own two feet, married or not.

Except her feet hurt. She wiggled them surreptitiously under the table and prayed no one else would ask her to dance, at least not for a little while. Feeling a presence at her side, she turned, glanced up and found Quinn smiling at her.

"Sabrina Donnelly, you're the second most beautiful bride I've ever seen, and I hope you won't be taking that amiss because the first was my own lovely wife."

She patted the chair beside her in invitation. "I'd love for you to tell me about her. Mac says almost nothing, and I haven't wanted to press him but I'm curious."

He sat down and gave her a long look from clear blue eyes that would have seemed just like Mac's had they not been so much warmer. "He's never spoken of her much, and when I've tried he changes the subject. The other boys aren't like that, but they were younger when it happened. Mac had the brunt of it. He adored his mother.''

"She must have been a wonderful woman.''

Quinn's face softened. A fleeting sorrow shadowed his expression but he took a breath and smiled. "Aye, Erin was that. She had a gentle strength all her own, not to mention a rare sense of humor.''

"She'd be very proud of her sons if she could see them today.''

"Oh, I'm sure she can. It's odd, you know, I was never a particularly religious man, but since her death I've felt her looking after us. I suppose some people would say that's just a reaction against the grief of losing her, but the feeling's there all the same and it's as real as anything I know.''

He was silent for a moment, then recalled himself. "But I've no call to be speaking of such things at a wedding. Have I told you how happy I am to have you for a daughter?''

"That's kind of you to say.''

"It's only the truth. Now would you mind a brand-new father, so to speak, wondering out loud why his lovely daughter seems a bit less than chipper this fine day?''

Sabrina made a mental note not to forget again that while Quinn might be softer in some ways than his son, he was no less keenly intelligent. "I'm just a bit tired,'' she assured him. "The last week's been a whirlwind.''

"Aye, I'm sure it has been, and you and Mac not knowing each other any time would be bound to add to the strain.''

No less intelligent *and* too perceptive by half.

"Are you saying you think we should have waited?"

He gave a sudden laugh and shook his head. "Oh, no, lass, that's the last thing I'd be saying. But I am wondering if perhaps you don't think that. Mac can be very…persuasive."

"Mac would give a bulldozer competition," Sabrina said flatly.

Quinn gave her an approving look. "Figured that out already, have you? It's true he's never shied from anything he wanted, but that doesn't mean he should be getting his own way all the time. That's not good for any man."

"In that case," Sabrina said, "I'm sure you'll be happy to know I have every intention of standing up to him. Marriage should be a partnership, a union of equals with no one person dominant over the other."

"Oh, absolutely," Quinn said, the quirking of his mouth belying the seriousness of his tone.

"I mean it," Sabrina assured him.

"I know you do, lass, and that's all to the good. The lad needs a challenge, best thing for him."

"I'm not interested in being a challenge. As I said, marriage should be a partnership—"

"Aye, a union—"

"Union?" Mac repeated. He'd approached so quietly that neither had noticed, but now he loomed very large—at least to Sabrina's eyes—and very compelling.

"That's right," Quinn said with a grin. He stood up and moved to one side. "Sabrina was just saying how much she approves of unions and all the good they do representing the working man.''

Mac eyed her with wary surprise. ''You didn't get that from your father, for sure. He's had even more problems with the unions than I have.''

On the verge of telling him Quinn was teasing, she changed her mind. ''You don't expect me to agree with him on everything, do you? Or with you, for that matter?''

His dark eyebrows drew together. ''No, of course not, I just wouldn't have thought you'd concern yourself with any of that.''

If her chin went up much higher, she was going to have a crick in her neck. Sabrina made a conscious effort to relax, but she couldn't entirely conceal her irritation. ''Business is business, whether it's construction or cooking. There are still a lot of the same problems.''

He looked amused by that. ''Somehow I think it's easier to get a soufflé to the table than to put up a fifty-story office tower, but maybe I'm missing something.''

''I'd say maybe you are,'' Quinn murmured from the sidelines. He grinned when the two looked at him, startled to see he was still there. With a quick wave of his hand, he was gone.

Mac sat down beside Sabrina. With so many of the guests taking advantage of the opportunity to get a few minutes with him, he had scarcely seen her in the last couple of hours. From time to time, he'd observed her talking or dancing with someone, and she'd seemed happy enough, but now he had his doubts.

"Are you feeling all right?" he asked. She did look somewhat pale and there was a flatness to her eyes that worried him. It occurred to him that putting a very large and elaborate wedding together on such short notice might have been more of a job than he'd realized. But she'd seemed perfectly calm and composed throughout the week, so much so that he'd found himself resenting her seeming imperturbability at the same time he was feeling anything but. With only hours left before he would finally have her to himself again, he had thought it prudent to keep some distance between them. Now, belatedly, he wondered if she was feeling neglected. Perhaps this hasty wedding wasn't living up to whatever romantic daydreams she'd had.

His mouth tightened as he wondered if she was storing up a slew of resentments to voice at the first opportunity. He accepted that she was spoiled. How could she not have been, given the way she was raised? He didn't even mind continuing to indulge her, but he wasn't putting up with any of the tantrums he was sure were bound to come, given how pampered and cosseted she'd been. She would just have to accept that.

"I'm fine," Sabrina said, but he barely heard her. Standing, Mac took her hand and drew her up beside him.

"It's time for us to leave."

Chapter 8

The car took them to Mac's apartment. Sabrina had been there only once during the previous week, just for a few minutes in the midst of all the hectic wedding preparations. She'd barely had a chance to even glance around and very little had registered except the thought, yet again, of how foolish she had been not to guess that Mac wasn't what he seemed.

Now, as the elevator door slid open directly onto the apartment foyer, she tried to gather her thoughts and take a look around, but that proved to be next to impossible. To begin with, she was exhausted. Too many nights with too little sleep had taken their toll. Worse yet, her mind overflowed with jumbled fragments—snatches of conversations, faces, bits of music, swatches of fabrics, menus, lists upon lists like some endlessly repeating reel of film that wouldn't stop until it broke.

Her head pounded, her feet throbbed and there was an ache in the small of her back that made her press a hand there and wince. The sudden realization of exactly how she felt—on her wedding night—was the last straw. Tears flooded her eyes. Horrified, she tried to blink them away, but not before Mac saw.

He cursed under his breath even as she dashed the tears away with the back of her hand. "I'm fine," she said just as she had while they were still at the reception. It hadn't been true then and it was even less so now.

"You're too damn delicate," he said gruffly even as he lifted her with great tenderness. He carried her up the wide staircase that led to the second floor of the apartment, then down a long hall to the master-bedroom suite. The room was in darkness, but the curtains had been left open, revealing the city bathed in the glow of a full moon and lit from within by uncounted stars.

Nestled in Mac's arms, her head against his broad chest and her ivory silk wedding gown trailing along the floor, Sabrina gazed out the windows. "So beautiful," she whispered almost to herself.

Mac started and tightened his arms around her. He found the view spectacular and never tired of it, but he would have expected Sabrina to think it commonplace. She was spoiled—wasn't she?—but apparently not jaded. He hadn't thought of the distinction before. Now he did, and was glad of it.

The fabric of his trousers stretched tautly over muscled thighs as he set her on the bed, then bent down beside her, cupping her chin in his hand. "You're worn-out, aren't you?"

She met his eyes, saw the unmistakable frustration in them, and felt a rush of pure annoyance. She would be damned if she would let him think her some weak little thing. "No," she said very clearly. "I'm not, and just for the record I'm not delicate either. Last year, I worked thirty-six hours straight preparing for a banquet in Paris, went back to where I was staying, took a shower and got on a plane to tape a video cooking course in London. That may not sound as tough as welding girders, but I'd still like to see you do it."

"No, you wouldn't." He let go of her chin and stood beside the bed, his expression inscrutable as he looked at her.

"Why not?"

"Because it wouldn't be a pretty sight. Would a shower help now?"

She had a sudden, flashing image of the shower in the cabin and blushed. Staring resolutely off to the left of him, she said, "That would be lovely."

A solitary shower, as it turned out. Mac turned on the water, made sure it wasn't too hot, undid the intricate row of buttons down the back of her gown and left her alone. "If you need anything," he said just before he closed the bathroom door, "yell."

Not that she was disappointed. Oh, no, far from it. A nice long, undisturbed shower was exactly what she needed. She stayed in it until the ache was gone from the small of her back and even her head stopped hurting. By the time she emerged, wrapped in a huge fleecy robe that she'd found in the closet beside the steam cabinet, and with her freshly washed hair toweled dry, she felt almost normal. Except for the butterflies that were doing aerial acrobatics in her stomach.

Determined to ignore them, she returned to the bedroom. A single lamp had been lit, casting a soft glow that in no way diminished the view through the still-open curtains, a view that stretched unhindered all the way across the dark swath of Central Park to the west side of the city and the river beyond. She stood for a few minutes looking out at it before turning back to the bedroom, which she studied with unrestrained curiosity. The spacious, well-equipped but ultimately rather stark bathroom had prepared her for furnishings that were luxurious but minimal. An immense bed set on a low dais faced the windows. Low tables on either side held lamps and digital keypads that upon closer examination, she realized, were controls. Yielding to impulse, she picked one button and pushed it, only to jump when the curtains began to slide shut. Pushing the same button again stopped them and a third push returned the curtains to the previous position. In quick order, she discovered more buttons that controlled the lights, ventilation and sound system. Yet another raised a TV screen from a concealing compartment built into one wall. Still more opened doors to a dressing area. She shook her head in amazement, contemplating the sheer number of gizmos and gadgets that had to be hidden away within the walls of the apartment. Trust a man to think of such things.

It had not escaped her notice that Mac was elsewhere. She wondered if she'd been mistaken when she thought him frustrated by her apparent weariness. After a week of not making the slightest effort to touch her, how badly could he want her really? Perhaps with the marriage, he already had all he wanted.

On that cheerful note, she took a firm grip on herself and went into the dressing room where she found the luggage that had been sent over for her earlier. Some kind soul had unpacked everything, and put it away neatly on the racks and in the built-in drawers. She found what she was looking for, removed the terrycloth robe and stared for a moment at the gown of almost sheer violet silk and lace before quickly donning it. Smoothing the fragile garment over her body, she avoided looking at herself in the mirror except for a single, fleeting glimpse that almost robbed her of courage. If Mac really didn't want her, her preparations would only add to the humiliation. On the other hand, if what she thought she had seen in his eyes was genuine, she had to wonder at the wisdom of inciting him yet further.

Caught between yearning and uncertainty, she eased the dressing-room door open and peered into the bedroom. Disappointment flooded her as she realized there was still no sign of Mac. Hard on that came anger.

Fine, if that was how he intended to be, let him. She would sleep alone and be glad of it. Never mind that this was the only wedding night they would ever have. Never mind that she didn't want to start their marriage alone in a cold bed.

The bedroom door opened. Mac stood silhouetted against a rectangle of light from the hall. Sabrina's breath caught. He had obviously showered elsewhere and was naked except for a towel around his lean hips. His still-damp hair brushed his massive shoulders that with his broad chest blotted out much of the light. She touched her tongue quickly to her lips and tried to still the trembling that swept her.

Mac stepped into the room quietly, his gaze on the bed. He expected to find Sabrina there and had told himself that if she was asleep, he would understand. He should have paid more attention to all she was doing during the week, should have realized how exhausted she was becoming. No matter what she said about not being delicate, he knew better. She'd been cared for and protected all her life. He didn't expect her to be otherwise.

His gaze narrowed on the flat, undisturbed surface of the bed, then lifted swiftly to scan the room. He relaxed slightly when he caught sight of Sabrina standing by the window, but his relief ended abruptly as his eyes raked her. Would the time ever come when he grew accustomed to her appearance, when the mere sight of her no longer made him instantly, almost painfully aroused? Sure it would, but when that day arrived, he wouldn't be alive to appreciate it.

With a wry sigh, he stepped farther into the room

and shut the door behind him. The soft lamplight and
the glow of the moon gave all the illumination he
needed to enjoy the vision before him. The gown she
wore hugged every inch of her delectable body. His
own hardened even further as he clearly made out her
nipples, the indentation of her navel and the shadowed
triangle between her slender thighs. With the greatest
effort, he raised his eyes to hers. What he saw there
startled him. She looked—surprised? No, it was more
than that, she looked uncertain and hesitant. As though
she had no idea what to expect from him.

Yet he was hardly a stranger to her, at least not
completely. Granted, their intimacy could be measured
in hours but, even so, surely she knew she had no
reason to be concerned.

Summoning all the patience he still had, and pray-
ing it would be enough, Mac crossed the space between them. He smiled and put his hands on Sabrina's
bare shoulders, his thumbs making lazy, circular mo-
tions. "Feeling better?"

She made a sound he decided to take as agreement.
She blinked once, looked away from him and quickly
looked back again. "I wasn't sure—"

"Sure about what?" he murmured, distracted by the
incredible silkiness of her skin and the warmth of her
body so close to his. For a week, he'd fantasized about
being with her like this, remembering every touch,
every caress they had shared. A very long, miserable
week that was, at long last, over. Or very soon would
be.

She lowered her gaze and took a quick, shallow breath. "It doesn't matter."

He rather thought that it did, but decided not to press her. The time could be better spent in other ways. Slowly, he slid one hand down her back as the other lightly caressed her arm. Urging her closer, he touched his mouth to hers.

"Did the shower help?"

"Hmm...what?" Her lips moved against his. She drew back slightly, her cheeks warming. "Yes, it helped. I'm wide-awake."

The smile he gave her was purely male and so sensuous that if she'd been exaggerating her claim to alertness a moment before, she most certainly wasn't now. Instinctively her hands flattened against his heavily muscled chest.

That was a mistake. Any thought of holding him off long enough to gather her wits promptly dissolved. Her knees weakened as heat flared deep within. The pads of her fingertips and the palms of her hands were suddenly acutely sensitive. The velvety roughness of his skin stretched taut over bulging muscles drew her irresistibly. Without pausing to think, she bent her head and lightly stroked her tongue over his flat nipple.

His response was instant and deeply satisfying. He groaned harshly and cupped her buttocks, locking her to him. The thick, hard pressure of his arousal wrung a moan from her in turn. Helplessly, she moved her hips against him.

It was more than Mac could bear. All his good—

not to say noble—intentions flew out the window and
went sailing away over the distant river. The week of
celibacy combined with memories of the most intensely satisfying sexual experience of his life had already raised his need to a fever pitch. Sabrina's instinctive, enthralling touch sent him right over the
edge.

He made a harsh sound deep in his chest and lifted
her. Half a dozen strides took them to the bed. He laid
her down and swiftly lowered himself, covering her.
Holding his weight on his forearms, he caught her chin
and kissed her long and deeply. His tongue plunged
wildly as he raked up her gown to her waist and thrust
his steely thigh between hers, opening her to him.

He meant to go slowly, to assure her complete
readiness, but with every thud of his heart and every
breath he drew, fire ran through his veins, driving him
on with urgency he could not resist, try though he did.
He slid his hands over her breasts, freeing them from
the gown, his dark head moving from one pale crest
to the other as he suckled and laved her nipples. Gasping, she tried to move but he continued to hold her
firmly beneath him, knowing that if he didn't, it would
all be over far too soon.

"Be still," he said thickly as he caught her wrists,
pinning her arms to the bed, and with his mouth raked
a line of fire down her body to the sweet apex of her
thighs.

"I can't," she gasped, struggling against him. "I
want...I need to touch you."

Her plea, uttered in a husky whisper, almost undid

Mac. He burned for her touch, but he was also determined to bring her to pleasure before he yielded to the incredible carnal hunger he had never felt before, not like this, not with any other woman. Their lovemaking in the cabin had turned out to be only a taste of what was to come. Desperately, his burnished skin sheened with sweat, he fought the all but irresistible desire to thrust into her again and again with no thought of anything but the lust that threatened to consume him.

If it killed him—and that seemed at least a possibility—he wouldn't do it. He couldn't, not to Sabrina. But heaven help him if he couldn't ready her quickly.

His hand slipped between her legs and he groaned with relief to find her hot and wet. Between clenched jaws, he said, "Sweetheart, tell me if I hurt you, promise me..."

Sabrina gazed up at the man who held her so intimately, seeing the skin drawn taut over his cheekbones, the smoldering glitter of his eyes, and felt the wildness explode within herself. She clasped his powerful shoulders, seeking some way to reassure him, but she had no breath, could not speak, could do nothing except obey the urgings of her body—and his.

He was already entering her and far from being dismayed her whole body arched bow-tight, her breasts rubbing against his chest and her hips rising to take him deeply and fully. Her slim legs wrapped around his waist, clasping him to her even as her inner muscles did the same. So complete was her possession, and so sudden, that Mac's senses whirled as a red mist moved over him.

His control was gone. Seated in her to the hilt, he plunged wildly, the convulsions of her release triggering his own.

Mac raised his head, awareness returning slowly. He was lying sprawled on top of Sabrina, his face buried in the crook of her neck, his hands still holding her against him, their bodies still intimately joined. His heartbeat resonated in his ears, and his lungs felt like heated bellows. Disbelief filled him. He had never succumbed to a woman so completely as to be made insensible by her. Never, that is, until now.

She had turned him into a mindless, rutting animal and he'd loved every second of it. Incredibly, the smile curving her lush mouth seemed to suggest she had, too.

Turning slightly, her gaze met his. He watched, fascinated, as her cheeks darkened. Gently, she brushed aside a lock of hair that had fallen across his forehead. Her fingers lingered, tracing the hard line of his jaw before running lightly over his mouth.

He said nothing but turned over onto his back, drawing her with him. His arms remained close around her, one sinewy leg thrown over hers in a position that was blatantly possessive. He nestled her head against his chest and stroked her hair gently. Absolute satiation blurred the edges of his thinking, but he marveled at how in the aftermath of such passion, he felt tenderness every bit as strong. He wanted to cherish and protect her, to keep her safe in every way. Quite simply, he wanted her to be happy.

With a jolt, he realized he was in very real danger of being held in thrall by a woman he could still barely claim to know and whose father he still regarded as an enemy. His hand fell away from her, his fists clenching against the bed. Inexorable sleep claimed him just then, but he slipped into it scowling.

Sabrina lay awake for a short time, soothed by the steady rise and fall of Mac's breathing. She felt dazed and bewildered, stunned by the intensity of her response to him and by the overwhelming sense of helplessness that swept over her whenever she was close to him. Slowly but relentlessly the fear grew in her that she was in very real danger of losing herself. Having only recently asserted her claim to an independent life, how could she let herself become so terrifyingly dependent on a man who was still, in some ways at least, a stranger?

The answer was obvious—she couldn't. However much she wanted to give herself to him completely, she had to hold back, to keep some distance from the hurt that would be inevitable if he truly didn't feel for her as she did for him. As hard as it would be, she had to be sensible. Something nagged at the back of her mind, some question about what really was sensible where love was concerned, but she couldn't catch hold of it. Nor did she try particularly hard, for in his sleep Mac instinctively reached out to her. Cocooned in his strong arms, sheltered by his powerful body, she surrendered to her dreams.

They left the following day, their destination the Channel Island of Jersey. For a week, they basked in

soft sea breezes carried by the Gulf Stream, walked in
startlingly tropical gardens, rode along cliff-strewn
shores and explored the ruins of medieval keeps that
seemed to dot every hill and bay. In the privacy of
their secluded residence, they gave free rein to the
sensuality that overwhelmed them both.

Nibbling on a fresh apricot whose sun-tinted hue
matched her own, Sabrina sighed deeply and leaned
back in Mac's arms. They were lying beside the azure
pool, replete from yet another explosive bout of lovemaking. The highly discreet servants had completed
their tasks and withdrawn to their own accommoda-
tions some considerable distance removed. They were
alone except for the inquisitive birds that flitted among
the surrounding trees and the occasional flutter of a
butterfly. The air was perfumed with the scents of hibiscus. Making the most of their privacy, neither had
bothered to don a swimsuit, nor had they withdrawn
inside when their play in the water fueled the hunger
that was never very far below the surface.

"I could stay here forever," she murmured, stretching languorously.

Mac chuckled and leaned closer. Watching every
nuance of her expression, he touched his tongue to the
corner of her mouth, catching the drop of apricot juice
lingering there. Despite the balmy warmth of the sun,
she shivered.

"Remind me," he murmured just before he stroked
his tongue over her lips, "to buy apricot futures when
we get home."

Her hands clasping his shoulders, she arched against him, gasping softly. "I didn't know you traded in commodities."

"I don't usually." He moved her under him on the padded lounger, easing between her legs. "But I think there's going to be a big demand for apricots."

Taking the half-finished one from her hand, he smiled into her eyes as he slowly, deliberately rubbed the succulent fruit over her distended nipples. Bending his dark head, he licked each with slow, painstaking care.

"No fair," she protested weakly. "You should be exhausted, done in, finished—"

He raised his head and grinned wolfishly. "Must be something in the water here."

Her gaze narrowed as she tried to swat him. He grabbed her hand and pressed it to his mouth, licking the soft inner skin. "Or maybe it's the air…or the food…or the angle of the sunlight…" With each word, he dropped light, teasing kisses down the length of her, pausing finally at the silken cleft of her thighs.

"Or maybe it's none of that," he said softly as his fingers parted her. "Maybe it's just one special woman."

She blinked, surprised, for as much as he praised the beauty of her body and the sensuousness of her response to him, Mac had said nothing of his feelings for her. He had said little enough now, but perhaps it was a beginning.

If she could get him to fully trust her, to let down

the guard she could still sense at every turn, then perhaps he would open his heart as she had hers.

If...

His fingers moved, followed by his mouth, and she thought of nothing for a very long time.

Chapter 9

The phone woke Mac. He turned over groggily, grabbing for it before Sabrina was disturbed. Pulling himself up in the bed, he rubbed a hand over his face. "Yeah?"

"Hi to you, too, big brother."

"Seamus?" Mac glanced at the clock, quickly computed the time in New York. It was after midnight there, just before dawn where he was. Weariness fled. He was instantly alert. "What's wrong?"

The younger Donnelly didn't hesitate. Succinctly he said, "Somebody's buying up our stock. Started around midweek but could have been earlier, we're not sure yet. They're working through the usual shell companies so it's been a little hard to track. We weren't really certain what was happening until today—I mean, yesterday. Sorry, it's later than I thought.''

Mac sat up farther as the words sank in. His voice was hard. ''You should have called me sooner.''

Seamus was silent for a moment. ''You're on your honeymoon.''

''That's not important if Century's under attack....'' He heard himself and heard more of Seamus's eloquent silence at the same time, and cursed inwardly.

''Never mind. Look, I'm sure you've been handling it as well as you could, but I need to know who's behind this and I need to know fast.''

''Gotcha. I've got a team working on it. All of us plus a few other people I thought could help.'' He ran down a list of hard hitters drawn from Century's law and accounting firms. ''We hope to have something in a few hours.''

Mac had to admit that everything he would have done was being done, but he was very far from comfortable. ''I'll call you as soon as I've lined up a flight to New York.''

''Maybe you don't have to come right back. This could blow over.''

''Oh, yeah, how exactly do you see that happening?''

''I see us finding out who's doing it and taking the usual steps to counteract. What's wrong with that?''

''Nothing, except I see it as a little more complicated this time, not to mention dirtier.''

He could hear his brother exhale sharply three thousand miles away. ''You're not thinking it's—''

But Mac was thinking exactly that. Rourk Talveston was behind this latest takeover attempt just as he'd been behind all the others during the past year. And he had seized a rare moment when he had every reason to presume that Mac wouldn't be paying attention to business. Or maybe he hadn't just seized that moment but had actually created it.

Thinking the worst wasn't even hard. On the contrary, it pushed all the puzzling little bits and pieces of the last few weeks together and made them fall into place neatly.

"Oh, no. C'mon, he's your father-in-law now."

"He's still the same son of a bitch he always was."

"Jeez, Mac, maybe you need to cut the guy a little slack. You come along, scoop up his daughter, marry her when the two of you have barely known each other a couple of weeks. If you ask me, he's been damn decent about everything."

"And why do you suppose that is, Seamus? Because he has such a warm, personal regard for me and was so happy to welcome me to his family?"

"Yeah, well, put like that—"

"I'll get back to you," Mac said and hung up. He sat for a moment on the side of the bed, forcing himself to breathe deeply and calmly, to defeat the red-hot anger rising within him. When he was satisfied that he was in control, he stood up and went into the bathroom.

He didn't so much as glance at Sabrina, asleep in the bed, still warm and rumpled from their lovemaking. He knew that seeing her just then, naked and replete, could only weaken him. With the shower on, he picked up the phone extension. The downward rush of water masked the sound of his voice as he began making calls.

"I don't understand," Sabrina said. It was several hours later. She had awakened to find the bed empty and an odd sort of tension in the air. Sure she was imagining the latter, she went in search of Mac. But in place of the lover who had filled her days and nights with ecstasy, she found a stranger in a dark business suit, finishing a quick breakfast as he leafed through a sheaf of documents.

He glanced up long enough to give her a cool, impersonal glance in response to her startled query. "I just told you, I'm flying back to New York. I leave in half an hour. You're enjoying it here, so there's no reason not to stay as long as you like."

"Stay...without you?" She wasn't sure he heard her, so absorbed did he seem in the papers. "I didn't realize you brought work with you."

He did look up then, but it was just another quick, hard glance. "I didn't. These were faxed to me this morning."

"I see...there's a problem?"

He shrugged and stood up, putting the papers back into a leather binder. "Just a situation. It's business."

"I gathered that. You have to cut short our honeymoon and go back to New York because of this 'situation'?"

A slight flush darkened the prominent bones of his

cheeks. "We were only planning to stay another week and, as I said, there's no reason for you to leave."

Her throat was so tight that it hurt. She had no idea what had happened to change him so drastically, but she was horrified with the results. As calmly as she could manage, she said, "I don't think a honeymoon for one would really suit me."

If he shrugged one more time, she was going to pick up the lovely crystal vase filled with lilies and throw it right at him.

"Do as you like," he said expressionlessly, "but I'll be at the office more or less constantly. No doubt, you'll be bored."

Bored? How could she possibly be bored when she was in the grip of white-hot anger? What could possibly be more involving than that?

"I'll risk it. Half an hour, you said?"

When he nodded, she turned on her heel and marched back into the bedroom. Precisely twenty-eight minutes later, she returned, dressed and ready to go.

Mac was standing in the entry hall. Beyond the open front door, Sabrina caught a glimpse of the car waiting in front to take them to the airport. She ignored her husband completely, busying herself saying a courteous goodbye to the housekeeper, chef and gardener who were doing their best to contain their own surprise at the premature departure.

Her deliberate preoccupation kept her from seeing the hot flare of his eyes as they swept over her. She was wearing a sleeveless linen shift of deceptive simplicity. It hugged her high, firm breasts and slender waist before skimming smoothly over her hips and long, tapered legs to midcalf. The length should have been modest, but somehow on Sabrina, it wasn't. He was struck by the unexpected—and undeniably erotic—thought that the tight skirt somewhat hobbled her, making it impossible for her to run. That he should even think in such terms astounded him, much less that he should find it suddenly, piercingly arousing.

"Get in the car," he said, taking her arm and directing her toward it. She stiffened but didn't protest. As she slipped into the back seat, he caught a glimpse of a slit that ran up the back of the skirt to above her knees. Her movement revealed silken skin lightly touched by the sun, skin he had delighted in caressing only scant hours before. She was so sensitive behind her knees. All he had to do was touch her very lightly there with the tip of his tongue and she—

He was going to lose his mind. By the time he got to New York, he would be stark raving nuts. Wondering grimly how his dear father-in-law would feel about dealing with an out-of-control madman, he settled back in the car beside Sabrina. Neither spoke on the drive to the airport.

Unwilling to wait for the less than frequent flights to the mainland, Mac had chartered a small jet. It took them directly to Heathrow Airport outside of London where they boarded a regularly scheduled flight for New York. As she stepped into the cabin, Sabrina realized they were the last to board. The attendant urged them into their seats with anxious courtesy and quickly took her own. Moments later, they were airborne.

Mac spent the flight reviewing the papers he'd brought along, receiving more through the plane's on-board fax, and making phone calls. He made those calls from the small business-services area near the cockpit rather than from the phone at his own seat. Slowly, as the hours wore on and he kept both his distance and his silence, Sabrina had to accept that he was determined not to let her know what was going on.

A slow, inexorable sense of dread began to grow in her. There was only one reason she could think of why Mac would behave like this. Something very bad had happened and her father was involved. She didn't want to believe it, in fact, did everything she could to convince herself otherwise. But the suspicion lingered. By the time they reached New York, it had hardened to virtual certainty.

She had to stop herself from asking Mac outright during the ride to his apartment. No, not his, theirs. They were husband and wife, partners, a team. She had to remember that even if he seemed in danger of forgetting it.

He got out of the car with her in front of the building but made no move to go in. "I'll be late," he said. "I may not get home tonight at all."

She swallowed against the lump in her throat. "All right, but if you do, please wake me. Sometimes it helps to talk things out."

The look he gave her suggested he couldn't think

of anything that would be less likely to help, or that
he would be less inclined to do. Without another word,
he got back into the car.

The apartment had the stillness of a place that
hadn't been occupied in a while. Yet there wasn't a
speck of dust on any surface, nor was the air even
stale. Clearly, the housekeeper had done her job. Sabrina kicked off her shoes in the foyer and with them
in her hand, walked slowly through the spacious living
room.

She stood for a moment looking out at the city, but
for once the view couldn't hold her attention. With a
weary sigh, she went through the formal dining room
to the large kitchen beyond. Not surprisingly for an
apartment of this kind, it was outfitted as well as the
kitchen of a small but select restaurant. Ordinarily, she
would have been happy to explore, but all she wanted
now was a cold drink and a couple of aspirin.

She found the first in the floor-to-ceiling refrigerator, the second upstairs in the cabinet in Mac's bathroom. Looking a little farther, she found another bathroom next to it along with a separate dressing room
that connected in turn to a guest bedroom as large as
the master bedroom itself. With a start, she realized
that the layout would be well suited to a couple with
a preference for separate quarters.

Her lips pressed together firmly, she closed the door
to the guest room. Whatever Mac's attitude at the moment, she was his wife and they were going to share

the same bed. Or at least they were whenever he deigned to return.

In the meantime, she was determined to keep herself busy. Jet lag always hit her hard, but she'd learned some strategies over the years for dealing with it. Resisting the urge to take a nap, she had a cool shower instead. Dressed in comfortable slacks and a blouse, she went back down the broad, winding stairs. Everywhere she went, she flipped lights on. In a closet near the living room, she found the control center for the sound system. Selecting a concert by one of Ireland's most popular groups, she set it for all speakers and soon had the apartment reverberating to the rapid-fire rhythm of flutes, violins and drums.

With their return not expected for another week, there were no fresh foods in the refrigerator. But Sabrina managed to find a decent soup in the freezer. She deliberately held her thoughts at bay while she fixed and ate a simple meal. When she was done, and had cleaned up, she picked up the phone, carried it back to the table, sat down and took a deep breath. Then she punched in a number.

In rapid succession, she called her father's offices, his New York apartment and the house in Greenwich. At each location, she was told the same: Mr. Talveston was not in, but if she would like to leave a message...

She did, but it wouldn't have been remotely appropriate for anyone else's ears. Instead, she settled for simply asking that he get in touch with her as soon as possible. When an hour had passed without results, Sabrina's patience was stretched to the breaking point.

The overwhelming size and solitude of the apartment was a weight on her already overburdened spirit.

For a time, she tried to take refuge in the library and was even briefly distracted by looking through Mac's books. He had thousands on hundreds of subjects. Architecture was an obvious interest, but history far surpassed it in the sheer number of volumes. Even more telling to her was that these were real books, the kind anyone could find at a bookstore or library, and they had the look of having been read. She'd been in too many homes where books were just one more pretentious decorating accent, their tooled leather bindings intended to be admired but never actually opened.

Under different circumstances, she would have been delighted to have nothing to do but explore the library. But waiting for the phone to ring made that impossible. When another hour passed and she still had heard nothing from Rourk, she had to face the possibility that he didn't intend to return her call.

She had no doubt he knew about it. No one in his position could afford to be out of touch even temporarily. He would have been informed within minutes. A daughter whose safety had always been of paramount concern returns prematurely from her honeymoon and her father doesn't even try to find out why? That was utterly unbelievable and just one more confirmation that he was behind whatever was driving Mac.

Perhaps they were in competition for a project and Rourk had tried to take advantage of Mac's absence to yank it out from under him. There was no doubt that would be dirty pool and she couldn't blame Mac for being upset, but it wouldn't be surprising. Her father had never hesitated to take any advantage in business that he could get. She could regret his doing that, but she couldn't see why Mac would blame her for it, too.

As the day wore into evening and there was no sign of him, she had to conclude that despite their marriage, Mac still saw her as Rourk Talveston's daughter, not as his own wife and certainly not as an individual.

An increasingly irate and hurt individual who, sitting alone in the cavernous apartment, could no longer deny that she had made a serious mistake.

Chapter 10

Mac left the conference room where the team was working and went back to his office. They'd been at it for hours. He needed some time to himself to absorb what was happening and plan his next move.

Talveston was good, damn good. He obviously had been in combats like this before, and he had the strategy down to a fine art. From what they could tell so far, he was working through at least a dozen shell companies. They thought they'd found them all, but they couldn't be sure. Others might appear at any moment. He had his tracks very well covered and he was moving fast.

Strictly speaking, nothing he was doing was illegal. But if he wasn't stopped soon, he would shortly be in a position to challenge for a position on Century's board of directors, possibly even to attempt to force it to merge with his own company.

Mac would see him in hell before that happened.

He caught his father's eye as he left the room. It surprised him how unworried Quinn looked. He'd been through this with Talveston once before, although on a much smaller scale back when both men were starting out. He'd lost then—badly—yet now he showed no concern that the same would happen to his son.

Indeed, the only thing that seemed to be bothering Quinn was that Mac had broken off his honeymoon to deal with this. He'd even expressed some concern regarding how Sabrina felt.

Quinn could worry about her all he liked, Mac was determined not to do so. He wasn't going to think about how she'd looked, standing there on the sidewalk, obviously strained, pale beneath her recently acquired tan. He had no reason to ponder what she was doing at that moment, if she was all right, if she had an inkling why he was acting as he was. Or if she had far more than an inkling, if she knew full well what was happening and why.

He wasn't going to think of any of that...except that he just had.

Grimacing, he closed the office doors and sat down behind his desk. The inestimable Liz Healey was in the conference room, a key member of the counterstrike team, but her handiwork was evident all the same. His desktop was completely cleared. She hadn't even left him something to fiddle with.

Now that he thought about it, Liz had given him pretty much the same look his father had when he arrived. That "are you sure you should be here?" look that said so much with just a raised eyebrow and a slight narrowing of the mouth.

It still amazed him. They *knew* what was happening, yet they seemed to think he should be lolling on a beach—or in bed—with a woman who might be a prime player in the attack on his company. They seemed to take it for granted that Sabrina had nothing to do with her father's actions. He couldn't understand how apparently sensible people could delude themselves like that, but if they wanted to, fine. He had no intention of following suit.

He rubbed the back of his neck, trying to ease some of the tension in the muscles there, while he considered his next move. Unlike many other construction companies, Century was in excellent shape financially and had a very large capital reserve. Talveston's runs on the stock over the last year had convinced Mac to keep a large part of that reserve very liquid for exactly the kind of situation he was facing now.

Century had begun buying up its own stock as soon as Quinn and the others realized they were under serious attack. Talveston still had the edge, but Mac was determined he wouldn't keep it for long. Eventually, what amounted to a bidding war between the two sides would drive the share price up high enough that one or the other would decide it was too rich and drop out. That wouldn't—couldn't—be Mac.

The problem was that he had no real way of gauging

how much Talveston was willing to commit to the battle. By the time the older man conceded, Mac could find his reserves drained, his stock overpriced to the point of being primed for a nosedive, and his company no longer anywhere near as solid as it had been. That just might be Talveston's real objective.

There was an alternative, though. To attack Talveston the same way. Mac had to decide whether to divert some of his own cash reserves to begin buying up Talveston stock. It was a key decision that might very well determine the outcome of the battle. Only he could make it.

He'd faced tough choices before, but never one wrapped in such an emotional tangle. If he failed to stop Talveston, he risked ultimately losing his company, which would mean betraying his family. But if he did stop him, he would hurt the woman who was his wife.

The very idea of having a wife was still taking some getting used to, yet he was surprised by how much he loathed the idea of causing Sabrina any unhappiness. Grimly, he steeled himself to do whatever he must.

Or at least he tried to. The effort was interrupted when his office door opened slowly and someone peered in.

Not someone.

Sabrina.

He was tired, worried, under a lot of stress, jet-lagged and probably a few other things as well. It wasn't her.

It was.

She stepped all the way in, turned around and closed the door with a click that seemed to reverberate through the office. He watched, still stunned, while she visibly took a deep breath, straightened her shoulders and faced him.

She smiled. Granted, it wasn't much as smiles went and it wobbled some, but it was a try all the same. "I thought you might be hungry."

Only then did he notice that she was carrying a picnic basket. Vaguely, he wondered where she'd gotten it. As far as he knew, he didn't own any such thing. Not that it mattered much when there was a whole lot more to wonder about. Like that filmy little dress she was wearing or the pain he thought he glimpsed in her eyes or if there was any way in hell he would ever learn to control his body's response to her.

His decidedly mixed feelings—caution, concern and lust—made him speak more gruffly than he'd intended. "You shouldn't be here."

For a moment, she hesitated. He saw the wave of uncertainty that went through her, saw, too, how she resolutely ignored it.

"I don't know why not. You have to eat sometime."

Despite himself, his mouth twitched. He admired her determination, but he also couldn't help but enjoy her innate gracefulness as she opened the basket, shook out a linen cloth and spread it over his desk.

"I know this may come as a horrible shock," he said, "but there's this thing called takeout."

She made a face but didn't pause, unpacking two

complete place settings, followed by an array of containers he had to admit looked interesting. Still, he persevered. "You've probably heard of some of it. Pizza, Chinese, burgers... Any of this ring a bell? We pick up a phone, talk and people bring food." He parodied doing just that.

The delectable aromas distracted him. As though by magic, glazed game hens appeared, garnished with slices of oranges, accompanied by fluffy wild rice and tiny green beans. Sabrina popped the cork on a bottle of Bordeaux, gestured to the meal and said, "This is food. The other stuff is filler."

"You're a snob," Mac said a short time later. He'd been hungrier than he'd thought, enough to finish one of the game hens and half the other in record time. The rest was good, too, but mainly it was the woman sitting across from him, idly twirling the stem of her wineglass between her slender fingers, who compelled his senses. She looked so damn beautiful and so enticingly feminine, it was hard to accept the strength he felt in her, yet it was there all the same. He would have to be a fool to forget it.

"A food snob," he amended. "If it's commonplace, it can't be good."

She took a sip of the wine and leaned back in her chair. "Oh, I don't know about that. I've had good pizza and some truly great Chinese food—Szechuan, mainly. I even had a burger one time I thought was incredible. However, you've got to admit most of the stuff is mass-produced glob."

"So what's wrong with that? Isn't glob one of the major food groups?"

She laughed suddenly, surprised, and for just a moment her eyes warmed. But then she caught herself and shrugged. "I suppose. So how's it going?"

If she'd expected him to be lulled by the food, wine and her company, she was in for a disappointment. The abrupt change of subject didn't faze him at all. At least not much.

"It's going and I think you'd better be, too. I've got to get back to work." He stood up, intending to help her pack up the picnic basket and ease her on her way.

Sabrina didn't seem to get the idea. Instead, she refilled her wineglass and took another sip before saying, "You can get back to work in a little bit. First, I want to know what's going on."

Mac dropped his napkin and slowly, without taking his eyes from her, resumed his seat. He let the silence extend until he saw her cheeks begin to pinken. His automatic response was to refuse to tell her anything. He never discussed company matters with anyone who didn't have an absolute need to know. She didn't, at least so far as he could see—or wanted to see.

On the other hand, barely a week ago they'd stood in church together and made vows to each other. Granted, nobody had said anything directly about trusting, but it sure seemed to be implied in all that love, honor stuff. New as he was to this married business, he didn't want to blow it right out of the gate.

But neither did he want to find out that his worst fears about Sabrina were true.

"All right," he said slowly. "We'll talk."

Sabrina folded her hands in her lap, hoping Mac couldn't see that they shook. Ever since walking into his office, she'd had to fight the urge to bolt. He was just too much—too big, too hard, too masculine, too commanding, too in control and too adept at leaving her with none. But he was also her husband, and she was damned if she was going to let him forget it.

She'd made a mistake letting him get all the way back to New York, dump her at the apartment and head off for his own private world without her saying a word. What a ninny she must seem, the meek little wife who did as she was told.

Time for Mac Donnelly to meet the woman he'd actually married.

"It's all well and good for you to hole up in this boys' club, man the barricades, damn the torpedoes and all that stuff. But we're partners now, and if you were counting on me to be a *silent* partner, you're in for a shock."

He'd just gotten it. This gorgeous, sensual, exquisitely female creature who kept him constantly teetering between the hotly sensual need to possess and the achingly gentle urge to protect was telling him...what?

"My father's up to something, isn't he? I figure that's the only explanation for what happened on Jersey."

"What happened?" Mac asked, watching her in-

tently. She was Rourk Talveston's daughter, all right.
He could practically hear the wheels turning in her
head, and there was a definite note of command when
she spoke.

"You, that's what happened. The guy right in front
of me with the inscrutable look and the hands-off attitude."

Until that moment, Sabrina really hadn't had any
real idea of what she would say to Mac, but now the
words just came of their own accord. She was angry
and it showed, but she was also desperate, fighting for
her man and her marriage. If she let him shut her out
like this, the damage might never be repaired.

"If you think I'm going to let you get away with
that, Mac Donnelly, you're crazy."

Before he could reply—or she could think better of
it—she got up, came around the desk, pushed his chair
back and bent over just enough to bring her mouth
close to his. There she hesitated, swept suddenly by
piercing doubts that threatened to overwhelm her.
What if she was taking entirely the wrong approach?
What if this only made him more distant, more cautious, more hostile? What if she simply couldn't pull
it off?

"I'm waiting," Mac said. Surprised, she glanced
down and saw that his hands were digging into the
arms of the chair, the knuckles showing whitely
against his burnished skin. She stared, fascinated by
those hands that were so large and strong yet touched
her with such gentleness. Unbidden memories rose.

She made a small sound deep in her throat and

moved just that much closer, inhaling the masculine scent of him, wool and soap and something else that was utterly male.

Her lips brushed his. He held himself absolutely still, letting her come to him, demanding nothing. Waiting.

Emboldened, Sabrina put her hands on his broad shoulders, feeling the heat and power beneath the smooth cotton of his shirt, and pressed a little closer. Her tongue probed, licking, tasting, savoring. Her senses whirled. She was very close to forgetting why she had come, what she hoped to accomplish. Just then, none of that seemed to matter.

"I love you," she whispered. So many times she had said those words in her heart, in the throes of passion, in its gentle aftermath, even just looking at him—whenever the fiercely tender force of her feelings for this man surged within her.

But she'd held back saying them out loud, hoping for some sign from him that he felt the same way. Now she simply couldn't stop herself and she didn't care. She was tired of control and caution, and too worried about the future to do other than follow her heart.

"I love you," she said again, trembling not only with passion but with unrestrained joy. Her hands cupped his lean cheeks as she deepened the kiss, taking his harsh groan as her breath. Mac remained in control for long moments, but quickly enough their shared ardor snared them both. His big hands clasped her hips, maneuvering her onto his lap. She felt his hardness beneath her bottom and couldn't keep herself from squirming in sheer pleasure.

"Don't," he whispered harshly, but with no conviction. A steely arm wrapped around her waist, another slipped beneath her buttocks. He lifted her, spreading her legs as he settled her facing him, straddling his heavily muscled thighs. He took control then, kissing her breathless, his tongue driving deep, his hands on her hips moving her against him in a rhythm that quickly made them both mindless.

When he broke off briefly and she felt cool air against her back, Sabrina was startled. So quickly that she gasped, the filmy organdy dress she'd donned to boost her courage fell away. Mac slipped her arms free and twined them around his neck before cupping her breasts. He rubbed his thumbs back and forth over her rigid nipples, continuing all the while with deep, blatantly carnal kisses.

"So sweet," he murmured. Rising partly, he pushed the dishes to the far edge of the desk, not heeding when several landed on the floor. Bunching her skirt above her thighs, he set her before him and undid the front clasp of her bra.

With a spurt of astonishment, she realized that he meant to take her right there on the desk. Far from being shocked, she couldn't deny her own arousal. Nor could she pretend even for a moment that she would refuse him anything.

Frantic with her own need, she yanked his shirt out from beneath his waistband and stroked her hands underneath. The touch of his bared skin was almost more than she could stand.

"Now," she urged. "Please Mac, now..." Her fingers went to his zipper, brushing the hard bulge beneath.

"Now, babe," he gasped and spread his legs wider, balancing them both even as he moved to free himself.

"Mac, we've got those new numbers—"

Seamus walked into the office through the door he'd just opened and froze. He stared in disbelief at the brother who for just an instant looked at him as though he had no idea in the world who he might be but if he took another step into that room he was going to die.

"Sorry," Seamus said quickly. "I didn't realize—" He started backing away.

With a wrenching effort of will, Mac got control of himself, if only barely. He lifted Sabrina off the desk, pushed the chair in front of him and settled her in it in a single fluid motion. When he turned again, she was effectively hidden behind his back, completely concealed from view.

"I'll be with you in a minute," he said. His voice wasn't quite as steady as he would have liked, but considering that his heart was trying to pound through his ribs, it didn't sound too bad.

Seamus looked at him as if he had to be out of his mind—for any number of reasons, including everything from the situation itself to the thought of breaking it off.

"There's no rush," he said and beat a quick retreat out the door, shutting it firmly behind him.

From the hall beyond, voices could be heard.

"He's busy just now, Padraic. He'll be with us soon."

"He said to bring the numbers the second they were in."

"Yeah, well, like I said, he's busy. It can wait a few minutes—"

"What's the matter with you, Seamus? You've gone beet red. Jeez, you're not coming down with something, are you? That's all we'd be needing."

"It's nothing, let's get back to work. Mac will be along."

"There's no other problem, is there?" Padraic demanded.

Whatever Seamus answered, it faded down the hallway and couldn't be heard.

Biting back the curse that threatened to explode from him, Mac faced Sabrina. She was curled in the chair, her arms back in the dress and the bodice pulled up over herself. Her hair was in tousled disarray, her eyes like the purple clouds of sunset. Her lips looked slightly bruised.

"I must be out of my mind," Mac said. He couldn't believe—absolutely could not believe—that in the midst of the most serious business crisis he had ever faced, he had come within seconds of forgetting everything to make love to his wife, on top of his desk in an office where he hadn't even thought to lock the door. What the hell kind of craziness was this?

What was happening to him?

''You have to go,'' he said and this time he left no doubt that refusal was not an option.

Nor did Sabrina even think to argue. She was deeply shaken by what had happened. She could hardly even bear to consider what had almost occurred. Another moment or two and Seamus would have walked in on them in the midst of—

She would never be able to look her brother-in-law in the eye again, but that wasn't really a problem because she'd just as soon crawl under a rock anyway. What insane, shameless—thrilling—behavior...

She took a deep breath, trying desperately for some fragment of calm. Mac seemed in considerably better shape—but then he would, damn the man. He must have a switch somewhere that he could turn on and off at will. Aside from a nerve beating in his jaw and a certain silvery sheen to his eyes that she had come to recognize, he looked completely unaffected.

Not her. She was still aching deep inside as he rode down with her in the elevator. He spoke briefly with his driver, giving instructions to see her home, then deposited Sabrina into the back seat. Before he closed the door, he bent down, cupped the back of her head and took her mouth with hard, fierce demand.

Barely had the kiss begun than he ended it, but it was enough to leave no doubt in Sabrina's mind that he was a whole lot more affected than she'd thought. Without a word, but with a very direct look that made her shiver all the way through, he closed the door and signaled the driver to go.

Sabrina was convinced she couldn't possibly hope to sleep, but she was wrong. The jet lag she'd managed to hold at bay finally caught up with her. Coupled with the sensation of riding an emotional roller coaster, it left her feeling as though she could scarcely set one foot in front of the other by the time she entered the apartment.

She just managed to stumble into the shower, dry herself off, pluck a nightgown from the dressing room and fall into bed. Her last thought before drifting off was that it was much too big a bed for one person. And much too lonely.

Chapter 11

I love you. She'd said it clearly, sweetly, hotly. He hadn't imagined it. She'd said it twice.

Mac caught his mind drifting in the same direction it had already gone countless times since Sabrina left. He'd never had problems concentrating, but now he seemed to have nothing but.

It was getting on toward midnight. He'd been working hard for over ten hours, but that was nothing. He'd gone a whole lot longer when there was need. The other people in the room had been grappling with the situation for days, not hours. They were the ones who had a right to be wrung-out and distracted, not him.

"I'm sorry, Eamon," he said. "What were you saying?"

His brother looked at him cautiously and repeated the point he'd just been making.

"We've only got a few hours left before London opens. We can hit Talveston there. He's vulnerable through that British subsidiary we found. Plus, he may not be expecting attack from that direction."

"We could do that," Mac agreed. "The problem is that subsidiary's pretty well buried. People won't know it's his."

Eamon shrugged. "What difference does that make? Isn't it enough that we know?"

Seamus and Padraic exchanged a glance. Quinn grinned. "Eamon, lad," he said, "Mac's looking to get the most bang for his buck."

When Eamon still appeared puzzled, Mac explained. "We can hit him where you say and Talveston will know we're doing it, but nobody else is likely to notice. If we're going after him, I want it out in the open where it sends a message to the financial markets in general. We need to leave no doubt about the lengths we'll go to in defending Century."

"I should have thought of that," Eamon said, abashed.

"Mac thinks of everything," Quinn said. "That's why we keep him around."

Maybe so, but he sure wasn't thinking too clearly at the moment. Seamus had kept his mouth shut about what he'd seen in Mac's office and nothing in his manner suggested he even had any memory of it. That wasn't surprising—Seamus was loyal to the bone—but Mac was grateful for it all the same. It would be a long time before he got over how crazy he'd acted, assuming he ever did.

He looked around at the people in the room. They'd sent the lawyers and accountants home several hours before. Even Liz had gone, somewhat reluctantly but glad all the same that there were limits to her responsibilities. What was left was the core, the people Mac knew he could count on to the end—and who could count on him the same way. Family.

Sabrina was family now.

Or she wasn't.

This was driving him nuts. He had to know.

He stood up and plucked his suit jacket off the back of his chair. Shrugging into it, he said, "I think we've done everything we can to this point. Let's all get some rest and meet back here at 8:00 a.m."

The faces around the table all mirrored the same surprise. Quinn spoke for them all. "We haven't actually come to any sort of conclusion, lad."

Mac was already at the door. He stood there, his hand on the knob, his big body very still beneath the deceptively civilized veneer. Without inflection, he said, "We hit Talveston when New York opens. By the close of the market, we'll have taken a large enough position in Talveston Enterprises to get his and everyone else's attention. There won't be any doubt what we intend."

Seamus whistled softly. "You're talking big bucks, brother. We'll have to put everything on the line."

"Yes," Mac agreed. "We will."

And with that, he left.

No car waited for him; he'd told his driver not to return after taking Sabrina home. That was just as

well. It was a nice night and he was in the mood to
walk. Century's offices were about two miles south of
his apartment. He turned onto Fifth Avenue, busy with
tourists and locals alike. Despite the hour, there were
still stores and restaurants open, and the clubs were
just starting to gear up. He heard half a dozen lan-
guages being spoken in the stretch of a few blocks.
The crowd thinned a little once he got out of the business district, but the streets were far from deserted. He
strolled along, hands in his pockets. The balmy air
soothed his spirits and made him realize how much
he'd needed some time to calm down and get his
thoughts in order.

All the same, by the time he reached the apartment
he was focused entirely on Sabrina and predictably
impatient. As he moved toward the bedroom, he reminded himself that she might very well be asleep.
He'd thought the same on their wedding night and she
hadn't been, but this time she was. In the light from
the hallway, he could make out that she was lying on
her side facing him, the covers pulled up to her shoulders, her breathing slow and steady.

He eased himself into the room, fighting the temptation to wake her. She had to be exhausted after the
trip home and everything that followed. It wouldn't be
considerate to wake her...or kind...or sensitive.

His shin went straight into a corner of the bedside
table. He groaned, the table clattered, the lamp on it
wobbled. He grabbed for the lamp, overreached and
sprawled on the bed, almost on top of Sabrina.

"Damn it." He managed to get the lamp back in place, but she was already sitting up, blinking in surprise and just a little alarmed.

"What—?"

"It's okay," he said quickly. "It's just me. I banged into the table."

"Are you all right?"

"Yeah, I'm fine." He got off her and stood, rubbing his shin. "I'm sorry I woke you. Go back to sleep."

"What time is it?"

"After midnight. You need more rest."

She didn't seem convinced. Instead of lying back down, she sat up farther, letting the covers drop to her waist. She was wearing a nightgown, but it didn't conceal very much. Mac looked away hastily. He wanted to be noble, but Sabrina was making it damn hard.

For his resolve and something else as well.

"Maybe I'd better sleep in the guest room."

"No!" She was out of bed in a shot, and in a tangle of silk and lace. Hands on her hips, defiance on her face, she said, "We are not having separate bedrooms."

He looked at her in amazement. "Of course we're not. Where did you get that idea?"

"From the way this apartment is laid out. There's a whole other bedroom suite." She tipped her chin in its general direction.

He loved that chin, loved kissing it, loved watching what she did with it when she was angry.

"That was there when I moved in," he said. "I didn't put it there."

Slightly mollified, Sabrina let her chin fall a notch, but she wasn't done yet. "Even so, I'm not sleeping in it."

"Damn straight you're not." The very idea appalled him. He hadn't gone to the extraordinary length of getting married to have his wife sleep in another room.

"No, I'm not."

They stared at each other. Slowly, Mac said, "Then what are we arguing about?"

"We're not arguing."

"We're arguing about not arguing?" He couldn't help it, he grinned.

Her hands dropped from her hips. She stood looking at him, her eyes very wide. As he watched, her tongue eased out to moisten her lips.

"That's it," Mac growled. He crossed the room in a handful of strides, wrapped an arm around her waist and pulled her up hard against him. "I was going to be considerate, I really was. But if you're going to stand there right in front of me and do that, you can't expect me not to—"

"Do *what?*" Sabrina asked, bewildered and breathless. His jacket was open. She could feel the steely heat of his chest against her breasts, her nipples already almost painfully aroused, everything she had felt earlier in his office returning with a vengeance.

"That thing with your tongue," he growled. "Your lips—" He didn't even try to explain further but simply took her mouth with his in a kiss she felt clear to her toes and right smack back up.

Her knees buckled. She sagged against him, held

upright only by his strength and her hands clasping his shoulders.

They made it to the bed but just barely. Their lovemaking was hot, fast and explosive. It was as though they hadn't stopped in the office but just carried right over. Afterward, they lay in a tangle of limbs and bedcovers, both breathing hard.

''That was incredible,'' Mac groaned. Sabrina's head lay on his chest. His jacket was gone, his shirt open. His pants were still on, sort of, but he'd kicked his shoes off. She was naked, the nightgown discarded on the floor. He vaguely remembered yanking it off.

He stroked her hair gently, his fingers twining in the silken curls. He could still feel the slowly receding tremors of passion that had taken him to unparalleled heights, yet even before they faded tenderness just as strong swept through him. He had an irresistible need to soothe and care for her, to surround her with gentleness and let nothing harmful ever come near her. He'd never experienced anything like it.

This feeling was something entirely different, vastly deeper yet at the same time exultant.

Love?

He didn't want to think about that. Later, when this business with Rourk was settled, when he knew where he stood with Sabrina, then he would deal with it. When it was safer.

Oh, great. Since when had he been too scared of anything to meet it head-on?

Since Sabrina.

"Look," he said quietly, "I think we really do have to talk."

She stiffened slightly but then raised herself up and met his gaze. "All right."

"First things first." He drew her back against him, holding her close, his hand brushing her back in slow, rhythmic strokes.

"Rourk's making a run on Century." She tried to sit up again, but he pressed her head to his chest. "It's okay, really. We've stopped him before and we will again."

She was silent for a moment. "When did this start?" Her voice was strained.

"Midweek, maybe a little sooner."

"Right after we got married, while we were on Jersey?"

He couldn't deny it and didn't try. "Seems that way."

"Oh, God—"

This time, he let her go. Her face was drawn, her eyes bleak. "How could he do this? He's trying to use our honeymoon to catch you off guard? To take advantage of our being married to try to hurt you?"

That was exactly what Mac believed, but he didn't see any reason to rub it in. "Who knows how long he was planning this. Probably from long before we met. It doesn't matter. We'll stop him same as we've always done."

"It does matter. He's my father, your father-in-law. If he had any regard for us, he wouldn't be doing this."

Again, Mac agreed but he hated the pain he saw in her eyes, relieved though he was to see it. Nothing in her response suggested she had known what Rourk was up to, much less that she approved.

She took a shuddering breath. "I thought he might be trying to get a job you wanted. God, that was stupid. I should have realized—"

"There was no reason for you to realize. He's your father, you love him. You wouldn't think something like this about him. Besides, it doesn't have anything to do with you. It's me he's after."

"Anything that has to do with you has to do with me. He should know that. I can't believe he doesn't." She shook her head in angry bewilderment. "I tried to call him yesterday. I left messages at his office, the apartment, the house. He hasn't called back and now I know why."

"I can see why he'd be ducking you," Mac acknowledged.

"He better go right on doing it, too." The anger was growing stronger, matching the pain. A possibility occurred to her. "Unless you want me to call him, insist that he stop."

"No, absolutely not. This is business and that's how it will be handled. Besides, I don't want to leave any thought in his mind that he could take us. He needs to know once and for all that he can't."

"How's he going to know that?"

"Because," Mac said quietly, "we're going to take him."

He didn't know when exactly he'd made up his

mind to tell her, but he'd done it all the same. He couldn't claim to care about their marriage and keep shutting her out the way he'd been doing.

"When the market opens this morning, we'll have buy orders in place for Talveston Enterprises stock. Instead of continuing to defend our own, we'll attack his."

"Isn't that risky?"

"There's an element of risk," Mac acknowledged. "Rourk could choose not to defend and instead keep buying Century shares."

"What would you do then?"

"There'd come a point where I'd have to break off and protect our own position. But I'm betting Rourk's ego won't let him ignore our hitting his own company. There have been runs against him in the past—not by us, by others—and he's always defended vigorously. He's very territorial in that regard. It's as though he can't resist. He may be able to hold off for a few hours, but when he sees we're serious, he'll start buying for himself."

"You seem very sure of that," Sabrina murmured.

"I'm depending on it," Mac acknowledged.

"I suppose this sounds horribly naive, but I don't understand why each of you can't just run your own company without getting in the other's way."

"Because we're competitors. We go head-to-head on virtually every job worth our attention. Your father doesn't like that. He was number one in this town for long enough to have gotten used to it. Ever since we've seriously challenged him, he's been looking for a way to do us in.''

She shook her head ruefully. ''And to think people say the haute cuisine world is a jungle.''

Mac coughed in surprise, then looked down at her silken head. ''People say that?''

''Oh, yeah, all the time. I could tell you stories... No, better not, you've got enough on your mind.''

She sounded serious. He remained skeptical. Apparently, she didn't understand the real extent of what was going on between him and Rourk. That was okay. He preferred her being sheltered. It was bad enough she had to deal with it at all.

''You can tell me,'' he said, glad she couldn't see his grin. ''I can take it.''

''Well, if you're sure... For instance, I was in a cooking contest a few years back where one of the guys I was up against tried to poison me.''

''What!'' She was exaggerating, she had to be. If she wasn't, he would have to find out who the guy was and go after him with his own meat cleaver.

''He laced my salad with pokeweed leaves.''

''Pokeweed? Doesn't sound like something you'd want to eat.'' It didn't sound too serious, either. He could understand her being upset, though. It was a lousy thing to do, giving her a bad salad.

''It's a really violent emetic, not likely to actually kill you unless there are complicating health factors or a small child gets hold of it, but it can sure put you in the hospital.'' Matter-of-factly, she added, ''Of course, the leaves actually can be eaten but only twice cooked, each time in clean water. Personally, I wouldn't do it, but some people will eat anything.''

"He tried to poison you." Mac was having trouble talking, probably because he wasn't breathing. He was too busy being insanely enraged.

Sabrina looked up, saw the expression on his face and her eyes widened. "It was years ago," she said quickly. "I didn't eat any of it. Better yet, I won the contest.''

"Where is this creep now? Just tell me where he is.''

"Uh…I think he shipped out for the Mars Colony.''

"We don't have a Mars Colony.''

"He's going to start one? Look, wherever he is, it doesn't matter. I wouldn't have mentioned it if I'd realized you'd react this way.''

"I'm supposed to be okay about somebody trying to kill you?''

"Not kill, just temporarily disable. I told you, it's a jungle out there. Your average restaurant kitchen is chock-full of lethal weapons, some of them walking around on two legs.''

"But you like it?" he asked on a note of wonder. His delicate little wife was proving to be full of surprises.

"I love it. I'm good at it, and I can more than hold my own." Smiling down at him, she added, "Really, there's no reason for you to be concerned.''

He wasn't convinced, but she'd finally managed

what he suspected she'd been trying to do all along, distract him.

"Speaking of love..." he said before his arms came around her and he drew her close.

This time, they even managed to get *his* clothes off.

Chapter 12

Mac was at his desk by 7:00 a.m. He used the extra hour to organize the buy orders he would issue throughout the morning, beginning when New York opened. It was just as well he'd given himself additional time. Despite his best efforts, his thoughts kept turning toward Sabrina. Well, not thoughts really, more like erotic images accompanied by hot, sweet jolts of passion that made it damn hard to concentrate.

Grinning ruefully, Mac decided that once this was over he would take his bride back to Jersey to resume their interrupted honeymoon. They would lie by the pool and eat apricots again. Or at least she would eat them, he would be satisfied to lick up the juices.

Thinking along those lines was definitely not going to make the day go any quicker. With a sigh, he continued putting his orders in place. By 8:00 a.m., activity on the executive floor was brisk. All the brothers were assembled, as were Quinn and Liz Healey. There was a "war room" atmosphere reminiscent of when they were putting together bids for major projects, only even more serious.

Mac joined them around the conference table.

"Good morning," he said. "Everyone set?"

Quinn nodded. "Set as we'll be. Eamon, Padraic and I will watch the ticker. If Century or Talveston hiccups, you'll know about it. Sean and Baird—" he nodded to the twins who grinned back, looking like a pair of wolf cubs eager for play "—will monitor the foreign markets, keep an eye on our interests there just in case Rourk tries a back door. Seamus is liaison to the funds managers. You can bet they'll be calling as the day wears on."

"I expect to do a lot of extra hand-holding today," Seamus said, then joined in with the general laughter over that. No one had to be told what would happen once Mac's plan became evident. Both Century and Talveston were popular stocks with various mutual funds. The people responsible for those would be sitting on the edges of their chairs, assuming they could stay in them at all.

"That's fine then," Mac said. He glanced around at each of them and was satisfied by what he saw. They looked ready and eager for action. He nodded once and reached for a phone. "Let's go."

The first wave of buy orders was in place when the New York Stock Exchange opened. Mac had given instructions for them to be funneled in over an hour

or so. He didn't want to do anything that would shock
the market and trigger the safeguards put in place after
the '87 crash. Slow and steady was the way to go.

Or so he thought until moments after the opening
bell when a curse broke from Quinn, swiftly followed
by the same from Eamon and Padraic.

"What the hell...?" the older Donnelly demanded.

Mac moved swiftly to where they were grouped
around the computer monitors that showed the con-
stant flurry of activity on the exchange. A quick glance
at the symbols told him everything he needed to know.

Barely had the opening bell died away than a massive buy order for Talveston swallowed up millions of
the company's shares. It also set off a buying frenzy
that over the next few minutes sent the stock price
careening straight up against the exchange tripwire.
Less than thirty minutes after the market opened, the
directors of the exchange cut off trading in the listing
for the day.

The group assembled in the conference room
watched it all happen, helpless to do anything to prevent it. For Mac, it was like standing on the sidelines
as an accident unfolded in slow motion. He followed
the rapidly flowing numbers with disbelief that slowly
but relentlessly turned to grim acceptance. There could
be no doubt what—or who—was behind this.

"Son of a bitch," Seamus said softly. Like the others, he looked shell-shocked. All their carefully crafted
plans lay in shambles around them.

As one, they looked at Mac, not with blame or fear

or even questions. Just with sympathy. Without him having to say a word, they knew.

All the same, Seamus wanted to be sure. He put a hand on his brother's arm and said gently, "Did you tell her?"

Mac nodded. He didn't trust himself to speak. Never in his life had he felt so bitterly betrayed—or so savagely angry.

Quinn let out his breath slowly. His face was flushed, but he spoke calmly. "He's her father, lad. She's bound to feel loyalty to him."

Mac swallowed even though it hurt. He welcomed the pain. It served to remind him of how incredibly stupid he had been. "Apparently so." He sounded hoarse. "She clearly has none to me." He couldn't stand to look at them anymore, to see how he'd failed them, to know what they must be thinking, Seamus especially who had the most reason to understand how in thrall his brother had been.

Had been. It was over now, burned out of him in a white-hot wave of fury and shock when he finally realized what was happening. As the anger receded, he felt strangely peaceful, as though a wall had come down between him and the rest of the world.

He glanced once more at the monitors and saw exactly what he'd expected. "Rourk is attacking."

It made perfect sense. Thanks to the preemptive strike of his massive buying order for his own stock, Rourk hadn't been forced to commit the amount of resources he would have needed if Mac's plan had been carried out. Instead, Talveston still had ample reserves to resume buying up Century stock.

Blessedly numb, Mac might as well have been on automatic pilot. His active, analytical mind took command, rapidly calculating their own position relative to Rourk's and extrapolating it over the next several hours.

One of the conference-room phones rang. Eamon picked it up, spoke for a moment and held out the handset to Mac. "It's the brokers. They were only able to execute about fifteen percent of your buy order on Talveston before trading stopped. Now they want to know what to do."

"There's only one thing we can do," Mac said. "Throw it all into Century. Shut trading down on our listing the same way Rourk did on his." He hated like hell to be forced to react to Rourk instead of act, but at the moment there was nothing else he could do.

As it turned out, not even that option was open to him. Three other phones in the conference room rang suddenly, all with calls from funds managers. Seamus was juggling handsets, trying to soothe each caller in turn when he suddenly paled.

"What is it?" Quinn demanded.

"There's a rumor the exchange is about to shut us down, citing unusual activity indicating we're in play."

"Damn it!" Mac grabbed the phone the brokers were on and rapped out an order. "Get that buy order through *now!* There's no time left."

None at all, not even enough for the few moments

the transaction would have taken. The group in the conference room watched in horror as trading in Century Construction was stopped, leaving them in a worse position even than they had been the previous day and with no way to respond.

"Rourk can't be happy about this," Quinn said when they had recovered enough to survey the damage. He looked at his eldest son with concern. Mac hadn't said a word. He sat slumped in a chair, staring off into the middle distance.

"It screws up his plans, too," Padraic agreed. "He can't acquire any more of us and we can't acquire any of him. Stalemate."

Mac spoke finally. He seemed to hear his own voice as though from a great distance. "Only until tomorrow morning. They can't keep us—or him—shut down longer than that. But in the meantime, he's holding a big chunk of Century and we've got nothing of Talveston to use against him."

He stood up, strode over to the floor-to-ceiling windows and looked out. With his back to the room, he said, "What do you suppose Rourk will be doing the rest of today? Sitting on his laurels or working the phones." He answered his own question. "He'll be on to every analyst and funds manager worth squat, and he'll sing the same tune to every one of them—he's sitting pretty and we're not. Come tomorrow morning, he's going to move in for the kill. Do they want to get hurt in the process or do they want to look good?"

"*How* look good?" Eamon asked.

"By buying Century," Quinn said.

Mac turned around. He glanced at his father, then at the rest of the group. "Right. He's going to tell them what they've already figured out, that he wants to take over Century and merge it into Talveston. He'll talk about what a great thing this will be, how together we'll be bigger and better than ever. The stock of the combined companies will go through the roof, they'll look like geniuses, and so on and so forth."

"So they'll be buying us tomorrow, too?" Eamon ventured.

"No," Mac said. "They'll be dumping us like crazy. We're known as an extremely well-managed company. They'll figure the first thing Rourk will do is get rid of anyone surnamed Donnelly, and they'll be right. They also won't trust him to deliver on anything he promises, which only goes to show that crew isn't as dumb as we sometimes like to think. Only in this case, they'll be playing right into his hands."

"They dump the stock," Eamon said, "the price goes down, making it easier for him to buy."

"Bastard," Seamus muttered. "But it'll be easier for us, too."

"Aye, there's that," Quinn said. "It's a calculated risk on Rourk's part, but it makes sense. It's better to be in a bidding war on a stock that's got some downward pressure on it rather than none at all."

"He's won this round," Mac said flatly. He walked away from the window, then headed for the door. "But there will be another tomorrow and we'll be ready."

"That's the right spirit, lad," Quinn said. "But

would you mind telling us how you plan to manage that?''

A pulse flickered in Mac's jaw. His eyes were flat and hard. "I wasn't entirely correct when I said we don't have anything of Talveston to use against him."

Quinn paled. He stared at his son. "Mac, don't... Listen to what the lass has to say, at least."

But he was through listening to lies. He was never going to listen to them — or her — again.

Sabrina held up the palm of her hand close to her mouth and blew hard. Iridescent bubbles floated into the air. She laughed and blew another handful, watching as one by one they popped. Long, hot baths weren't generally her favorite activity, but today she was making an exception.

After seeing Mac off to the office, she decided to do absolutely nothing but wallow in the sensual daze he'd left her in. She refused to think about her father, what he was doing, or anything at all along those lines. Mac had said he would take care of it, and she believed him completely. Glancing at the small clock on the counter by the sinks, she saw that the market had been open for more than an hour. It might be over already.

How wonderful that would be. Eventually she would think about talking with her father again. She had no intention of letting this cause a complete estrangement, but neither did she believe she would be able to forgive him entirely. He'd done a despicable thing with no thought for the consequences to her or anyone else. But first and foremost, she wanted Mac to herself for a while longer.

They needed a chance to get to know each other. Everything had happened so quickly between them, and they had so much catching up to do. Much of the small but fascinating things lovers learned about each other before they married still remained for them to discover.

Her thoughts were interrupted by the sound of a door opening somewhere in the apartment The housekeeper was due sometime during the day, but Sabrina didn't think she'd arrived yet. Besides, the sound seemed to come from the bedroom suite.

She waited, wondering if she hadn't been mistaken, until she heard footsteps right outside the bathroom door. Thinking the housekeeper was checking to make sure she had everything, she called out, "I'm in here, Mrs. Valdez. I'll be out in just a few minutes."

She was looking forward to meeting the woman again after being briefly introduced to her just before the wedding. Maybe they could go through the kitchen together, see if anything needed to be added. Mac had said the housekeeper did some simple cooking but didn't seem to enjoy it much. He hadn't cared enough—or eaten enough—to mind. Sabrina was actually relieved by that. She was looking forward to working in the kitchen, but wouldn't have wanted to displace someone who really enjoyed it.

Only it wasn't Mrs. Valdez outside the bathroom door. It was Mac. He walked in with a look on his face that instantly froze Sabrina in place. The skin was pulled tautly over his features, his eyes glittered and his mouth was drawn in a thin, cruel line.

''Mac...what's wrong?''

''Get out of the tub.''

His hands were clenched into fists at his sides. Never mind how well she did or didn't know him, she had no doubt that he was fiercely angry. She'd seen that look briefly the night before when she'd told him about the pokeweed incident. Then it had been directed toward a stranger. Now it was aimed straight at her.

Instinctively she sank lower in the bath as though the water somehow offered protection. ''I don't understand....''

''I said get out.'' This time he didn't wait for her to comply. He walked over to the tub, took hold of both her arms, and hauled her upright. Barely had her feet touched the carpeted floor than he jerked his hands away, as though he couldn't bear to touch her.

For just a moment, his eyes ran over her with insulting thoroughness, then he grabbed a towel off the heated rack and threw it at her. ''Dry yourself off and get dressed. We're leaving.''

Sabrina held the towel against herself but otherwise did nothing except stare at him. He looked like a complete stranger—his rage and contempt barely in check.

Gathering all her courage, she said, ''I'm not going anywhere until you tell me what's wrong.''

His mouth twisted. He came toward her, not stopping until they were scant inches apart. ''Oh, you're going, dear *wife*. If I have to drag you out of here in nothing but that towel.''

"Going where?"

"Somewhere your father's not going to be able to locate you."

The light in his eyes made her shudder. "There aren't going to be any more middle-of-the-night chit-chats, sweetheart. That is when you called him, isn't it? I don't think you would have waited to do it while you were fixing that charming little breakfast for me. He would have needed as much lead time as he could get."

Sabrina was shaking her head even before he finished. "I don't know what you're talking about. I told you I'd called Rourk, but it wasn't in the middlle of the night. It was shortly after we got back and he never returned the call."

"Stop it." The words were uttered almost quietly, but Sabrina didn't mistake the fury behind them. Mac looked like a man on the edge of a precipice and about to step straight over.

"Let me get dressed," she said. He didn't move, but he did let her go around him. She quickly grabbed clothes from the dressing room, but when he saw what she was choosing, he took them from her, tossed them on the floor and began going through the racks himself.

"You'll never make it if you wear those," he said, gesturing to the delicate silk pants and top she'd selected. "Wear these." He thrust a pair of jeans and a shirt into her hands, then added a sweater.

Looking at the last item, she said, "But it's summer."

"Not where we're going. Now get dressed."

Biting her lip, she took underwear and socks from a drawer, but when she tried to return to the bathroom, Mac stopped her. "Do it here."

Ordinarily she wouldn't have hesitated to get dressed in front of him. But this was horribly different. She felt acutely self-conscious and exposed. "I'd just like a little privacy."

"No." He folded his arms over his broad chest and leaned against the dressing room wall, as though daring her to object further.

Sabrina didn't bother. She was too angry herself and too hurt. If he wanted to behave like a total jerk, let him. The sooner she did as he said, the sooner she was likely to find out what was behind all this.

And the sooner she would be able to let him have it.

Even so, as she leaned forward to pull her panties on, she had the misfortune of catching his eye. The hot touch of his gaze sent a jolt of excitement through her that made her cringe. She straightened quickly and finished dressing as hurriedly as she could.

"If we're going to be away overnight, I should pack a few things."

He hesitated and she thought he was going to refuse, but finally he opened a small door within the dressing room and selected two pieces of luggage. The same two they had used for the trip to Jersey.

He packed for himself with the same efficiency that

he did everything else and was done in minutes. Sabrina was still fumbling with clothes, hampered by her ignorance of where they were going or for how long, and even more by the fear growing in her with each passing moment.

She hated the very thought of being afraid of Mac, yet she couldn't prevent it. Nor did she have any doubt that he was deliberately engendering that emotion in her.

"Don't bother with the nightgowns," he said when he saw her about to add several. "You won't need them."

Leaving it to her imagination to figure out why, he tucked her suitcase under his arm, took his own in one hand, and with the other hand guided Sabrina from the room. "Let's go."

Chapter 13

Mac did not, as Sabrina had half expected, take her back to the cabin in the woods. Despite the cold silence that had replaced his hot rage shortly after they left the apartment, she would have welcomed such a destination, filled as it was with memories of their first lovemaking.

Instead, they went by car to the airport. Mac drove them himself. There was no sign of his chauffeur. Once there, he continued beyond the usual terminals to a small one set apart from the rest. Parking behind it, he handed Sabrina out of the car, took their luggage and spoke briefly with a man who came out to greet them. After an exchange of no more than a few words, the man took the luggage and went off toward a hangar. Mac and Sabrina followed.

"We're flying somewhere," she said, not happy to

be stating the obvious but still hoping he would relent enough to tell her where they were going.

He didn't. Moments later they were in a small jet, the kind typically used by companies to ferry their executives around.

"Sit down and get your seat belt on," Mac said. He secured the door and headed for the cockpit. To her surprise, he didn't just have a few words with the pilot and return. Instead, it appeared *he* was the pilot. He slipped into the control seat, donned a headset, and proceeded to completely ignore her while he spoke with the tower, then taxied into position. There was a line waiting to take off, but it moved swiftly.

Once airborne, Mac made no move to return to the cabin even briefly. Sabrina was tempted to try to talk with him, but she suspected any attempt would be futile. It might be better to wait until his temper had time to cool.

Meanwhile, she tried to imagine what could have happened. Clearly, Mac's strategy to deal with her father had failed. Rourk had done something—known something—and Mac believed it was because Sabrina had told him...what?

Abruptly, she realized what it had to be. Mac had confided in her his plans to make a large purchase of Talveston stock. Rourk must have prevented that somehow, leading Mac to the conclusion that he'd been tipped off...by Sabrina.

Dismay filled her. If it were true, she could well understand why he would be in such a fury. He must be feeling savagely betrayed. Her heart tightened as she fought the urge to go to him and offer comfort. But he would only throw it back in her face. Besides, there was the matter of him completely failing to trust her, to have even the smallest degree of faith in her as a person and a wife.

How could he actually think that she would violate her husband's trust? If he believed her capable of that, he didn't know her at all.

That realization hurt badly but it didn't surprise her. She'd known how much they needed to learn about each other. Now she accepted that there was even more beneath the surface than she'd thought. Mac clearly still saw her as Rourk Talveston's daughter, with all the suspicion that prompted. If it was the last thing she did, he was going to see her as a person in her own right.

And as his wife.

She stayed in her seat throughout the flight, but she did look out the window from time to time to get some sense of their direction. From what she could tell, they appeared to be flying north. She had no idea of the plane's airspeed, so she couldn't calculate the distance, but by the time they began a slow descent she was sure they had traveled at least several hundred miles.

They landed at a private airfield unmarked except for a paved landing strip and a small hangar set beside it. No one was in sight. Mac taxied directly up to the hangar, killed the engines and got out. As Sabrina watched through the window, he took a key from his pocket and used it to open the doors of the hangar. He disappeared inside, emerging a moment later driving a pickup truck. He parked it beside the plane, went back inside the hangar and returned with a small tractor. She lost sight of him as he hitched the plane to it, then reappeared to carefully maneuver the jet into the hangar. That done, he came onboard again and gestured to her. "Get in the truck."

Sabrina obeyed without a word. She wasn't about to argue with him. Let him make whatever he would of her silence, it was the best weapon she had to eat away at his anger and make him let down the wall he'd set between them at least enough for her to try to get a few words through.

Until then, she would do what she had to because she had no choice, but she wouldn't make it one bit easier on him.

He loaded the luggage into the truck, relocked the hangar doors and took his place behind the wheel. Not a word was spoken during the hour-long drive that followed.

Sabrina had thought it cool at the cabin, but wherever they were it was downright cold. She supposed they were at an even higher elevation because the mountains in the near distance were snowcapped even though it was summer. Despite herself, she shivered.

"Shut the window," Mac said.

Surprised that he'd noticed her discomfort when she would have sworn he hadn't even glanced her way, Sabrina raised the window. It helped some, but she was glad when the truck's heating system finally kicked in.

They continued to climb, the air growing steadily colder and the view ever more spectacular. Finally, they came to a stop in a clearing. Mac killed the engine and got out. Sabrina followed more slowly. She looked around but could see only pine trees. There was no sign of any habitation.

Her gaze went to Mac. He had opened the suitcases and was busy stuffing their contents into backpacks that must have been in the truck all the while.

"What are you doing?" she asked.

He spared her one quick glance, nothing more, but he did answer, after a fashion. "Unless you want to haul a suitcase up that mountain, I suggest you get over here and finish doing this pack."

Sabrina looked up the mountain that seemed to rise perpendicularly not far from where they were standing, and gulped. "I've never done any climbing."

"And you're not going to now, at least nothing serious."

When she still hesitated, he unbent enough to add, "Just stay on the trail and do what I tell you."

"What I'm really tempted to do is sit down and not move another inch."

He shrugged. "You can do that, too. But it will be dark soon and very cold. You don't have any sleeping gear or matches or food. You'd be lucky to make it to morning."

He sounded as though he didn't really care. Sabrina blinked back tears. She would be damned if she would give him the satisfaction of seeing her cry. Stomping over to the truck, she stuffed her belongings into the pack by the handful, not caring whether she was wrinkling everything beyond repair. When she was done, she checked the straps, shortened them and put the pack on. To her relief, it was fairly light. She was sure she wouldn't have any problem carrying it.

An hour later, she wasn't so sure. They had walked steadily from the clearing, Mac setting a rapid pace. When Sabrina lagged behind, he reminded her yet again that it would be dark soon. She picked up her feet then, but glared at his back every step of the way.

The so-called trail was a barely distinguishable track that seemed to include every gnarled root and boulder on the mountainside. Sabrina lost track of how many times she stumbled. Once she went down altogether but managed to scramble upright without Mac's help. He had held out a hand but she'd ignored it, and when he asked if she was all right, she'd just glared at him and refused to answer.

There was some pride in that, at least, but very little in anything else. Too quickly, she ached in every muscle. Her legs felt as though they weighed at least a ton each and she was frantically trying to remember what she'd packed that could possibly weigh so much.

Still, she wasn't about to ask Mac for help. She would walk until she dropped before she would even consider doing that. So intent was she on getting through one step and the next and the next that she didn't see him glancing over his shoulder or notice the worried frown that creased his forehead as he saw her flagging.

When he suddenly appeared beside her, she started. ''Give me the pack.'' He didn't wait but took it from her, slipping one strap over his shoulder as though it weighed no more than air. Gesturing with his head, he added, "Come on."

It was a little better after that, but not much. Granted, the trail did take the easiest way up the mountain but in order to do that it had to wind around and around, adding miles to the trek. Sabrina was beyond tired when Mac suddenly stopped. She raised her head slowly and looked around.

The sun was going down in splendor far to the west. She could see it glowing fiery red in the cleft between two distant mountains. The sky was streaked with clouds of pale green, violet, lavender and orange. To the east, the first stars had already appeared, visible against an incredibly clear sky untouched by the haze or light pollution of the city. As she listened, an owl called softly.

The beauty of the place was so great that it brought a lump to her throat. Or maybe the air was so thin she was having trouble breathing. Not sure which it was, or caring, Sabrina noticed the small cabin just ahead. To her great relief, it appeared in considerably better repair than the cabin Mac had brought her to several weeks before. She stared at it in amazement, wondering at the effort needed to drag any quantity of building materials up the side of the mountain.

"They brought everything in by chopper," Mac said as though reading her thoughts.

Sabrina nodded numbly. "Makes sense. You have a thing for cabins, don't you? So why not build one in a place so hard to get to you have to use a helicopter to do it?"

"Not that it matters, but it isn't my cabin. I'm just borrowing it."

"Who from?" She didn't especially want to know, but at least he was talking. It was a start.

"A friend of Seamus's. He's away for a while fulfilling a lifelong dream to hike across Antarctica." With a glance at her, he added, "That's the kind of dream a man ought to stick to. It's a hell of a lot safer."

He didn't say safer than what, and she didn't ask. The answer was all too obvious.

Despite the exertions of the hike, Sabrina was trembling visibly from the cold. She followed Mac into the cabin without a word, but there was little relief to be found. The interior was as cold as outside.

Mac dropped the packs in the middle of the floor. "I'll get a fire started."

She nodded mutely, not trusting herself to speak. Her teeth were chattering too much. With sunset, the temperature was plummeting.

"There are blankets in a chest over there," he said. "Put one around yourself."

She did and felt better shortly. By the time he had a roaring fire going, the blanket was barely needed. But whether it was the cold, the hike or perhaps the complete upheaval of her life, Sabrina found she could barely keep her eyes open. She stared into the fire until she caught herself nodding off, then snapped awake.

"Is there any food in this place?" she asked.

"Only dehydrated and canned, but we'll manage."

"Oh, goody." She knew she sounded churlish, but she couldn't help it.

"You're too concerned with creature comforts. It will do you good to do without some for a while."

She glanced at him sharply. "How long a while?"

"As long as it takes."

Okay, apparently he wanted to play Twenty Questions.

"Takes to do what?"

"To get your father to agree—legally and in writing—that he will stop all attempts to take over Century."

As the full meaning of his words sank in, Sabrina's mouth dropped open. Slowly, she said, "And what are you offering him in return exactly?"

"His daughter—on a silver platter, if that's what he wants. It doesn't matter to me. God knows, I've got no use for you."

She bit her lip so hard she tasted blood. "Damn you."

Mac looked at her bleakly. So quietly that she could barely hear, he said, "You already have."

Neither spoke for a long time after that. After a while, when Sabrina didn't move but just sat staring into the fire, Mac got up and went into the small kitchen. He came back with a tray containing steaming bowls of stew as well as several different kinds of crackers and glasses of springwater.

When Sabrina ignored the food—and him—he pressed a bowl into her hands. "Eat."

She obeyed because it was easier than arguing with

him. If she argued, he might touch her and she didn't want him to do that. Not ever again.

What was that old saying? Marry in haste, repent at leisure. She'd done the first and she would have the rest of her life for the latter. She might as well get started.

When she was finished eating, she pulled the blanket more snugly around herself, stretched out in front of the fire and closed her eyes. The weariness that overwhelmed her was like a black weight holding her down.

She didn't even try to resist it, wanting it to push her into forgetfulness, if only for a little time. But it didn't work, or at least not entirely. She floated in some halfway place between consciousness and dreams, her mind drifting through snatches of memory.

Mac coming toward her that first day on the construction site, his chest bare and streaked with dirt, a fire in his eyes when they swept over her.

Mac on the soccer field, watching him with her heart in her throat, so afraid that he might be hurt.

His face above her the first time they made love, his powerful features taut with restraint as he brought her to shattering pleasure before finally yielding to his own.

Dancing with him at their wedding, walking, talking, laughing on Jersey. Jersey with the pool and the apricots.

Tears slipped unheeded down her cheeks. She wasn't aware of them, but Mac was. He watched the silvery trails of moisture against her pale skin for all of ten seconds before the almost superhuman control he'd been exercising broke.

He couldn't stand this. What he'd intended as a way to punish her for what she'd done had turned into his own hell. He hated seeing her sad or afraid or just worn-out. The need to keep her safe from all possible harm swamped whatever desire for vengeance he'd ever possessed.

He knelt down beside her, gathered her into his arms and carried her to the small alcove that held a pine bed. When he laid her against the still-cool sheets, Sabrina shivered. Instinctively, she curled herself more tightly. Mac stood next to the bed for several moments and when she shivered again, he couldn't ignore it. The last thing he wanted was for her to get sick. He told himself he was just being practical even as he knew that was a lie.

With a sigh, he undressed down to his briefs, then steeled himself to remove Sabrina's clothes. He got as far as her underwear before deciding he couldn't go any further. Getting into bed beside her, he drew her into his arms. She continued to shiver but not for long. Soon enough, the heat of his body warmed hers and she relaxed into deep sleep.

A sound she couldn't identify woke Sabrina. She lay in the bed, wrapped in stillness, and felt the warmth of sunlight against her eyelids. Felt, too, the lingering tenderness in her muscles that was more surprising than unpleasant. Only gradually did memory return and with it echoes of the previous night's bleakness. But even that seemed somehow lessened, as though a few hours of real rest and the coming of a new day made it impossible to entertain true despair.

She sat up, curious about a great deal all at once. Where was Mac? What was he doing? Was he still so implacably set against her? Was there any chance she might be able to talk some reason into him? Should she even try?

Anger energized her. Damn the man! He'd condemned her on the flimsiest possible evidence, virtually thrown away their marriage and now he seemed to think he was going to use her as a pawn to get what he wanted in business.

When hell froze.

She got out of bed, surprised for a moment to find herself so scantily dressed, grabbed up her clothes and marched into the bathroom. A short time later, she emerged, dressed, her face freshly scrubbed and the light of battle in her eye.

There was no sign of Mac. Very briefly, she entertained the possibility that he had left her. Her stomach plummeted but she forced herself to stay calm. He might have deserted her, it actually would have been a smart move. Even if she did manage to find her way back down to the clearing, the truck would be gone. She would have no way of reaching the airstrip or anywhere else. Simple self-preservation would dictate that she stay right where she was.

And plot the horrible tortures she would inflict on him when she finally got out.

She heard the strange sound again, the one that had awakened her. It was a series of clicks and it was coming from around the back of the cabin.

Sabrina went outside, taking note that it was a spectacularly beautiful day and warm enough so that she was comfortable in just a sweater. Coming around a corner, she stopped dead. Mac was there, his big, powerful body clad in jeans and a plaid shirt, his ebony hair pulled back at the nape of his neck to reveal hard, chiseled features. He was standing beside what looked like a portable satellite dish, and in the act of lowering the antennae of the cell phone he held in his hand.

''Good morning,'' he said when he caught sight of her.

Staring at the high-tech equipment that looked decidedly incongruous out in the middle of nowhere, she ignored the greeting. ''What are you doing?''

''Checking in with the office.'' At her startled look, he shrugged. ''You didn't think I'd be out of touch, did you? That wouldn't fit in with my plans.''

His stupid, hateful, hurtful plans.

''Have you talked to my father?'' she asked.

His eyes were shuttered, revealing nothing of his thoughts. ''He's been informed.''

''You bastard.'' She was so angry now that she could barely speak. The words had to be forced from her throat. ''You know the nightmare Rourk has lived with since my mother's kidnapping. You've picked exactly the worst spot to drive the knife into him.''

''No!'' That single syllable cracked like a rifle shot, sending the birds in the nearby trees fluttering into the air. With a visible effort at controlling himself, Mac said, "Precisely because I do know that, your father has been given every assurance that you aren't in any danger. Not one hair on your precious head is at risk. You're just going to be kept out of circulation until he agrees to my terms." With a grim parody of a smile, he said, "I suggested he think of it as your being on a spiritual retreat, a chance to reflect on your behavior and maybe come out the better for it."

"The better? The better!" That was it. She absolutely couldn't take any more of this. Marching up to him, she jammed a finger into his chest, emphasizing every word she said. "You arrogant fool! It's not me who needs to change, it's you! We made promises to each other, damn you! I've kept mine, you haven't."

Mac grabbed her hand. He didn't hurt her. On the contrary, at his mere touch a bolt of pleasure shot through her. His eyes narrowed. He let go of her but continued to stare at her warily.

"You set me up from the beginning," he said. "You dangled the bait—your own sexy little self— and I took it hook, line and sinker. Tell me something, did the plan involve marriage all along? Or were you just figuring to get close to me and use whatever you could find out?"

He leaned closer to her, his breath warm on her cheek. "When did you decide you wanted more? When you found out how good we are in bed? How I can make you moan and cry out, and beg me to take you?"

She hit him. She drew her hand back and hit him

with her opened palm right across the face. She'd never done anything remotely like that in her life and she wasn't very good at it. He didn't even flinch. She felt sick. With a low cry, she turned and walked— pride wouldn't let her run—back into the cabin.

Mac stayed outside for several hours. She didn't know what he was doing and she didn't care. Her emotions were raw, she was never far from tears, and she alternated between wanting to wring his neck and plead with him for forgiveness for something she hadn't even done.

He finally came into the cabin around noon, saw her sitting in front of the now-cold fireplace and frowned. He went into the kitchen but returned at once.

"You haven't eaten anything."

Sabrina ignored him. If she pretended he wasn't there, she could pretend none of this was happening.

He waited long enough to realize that she had no intention of answering, cursed under his breath and went away again. A few minutes later, he came back with a tray of food.

"You have to eat."

He stood over her, waiting for her to comply. She didn't move. Not by a glance, a word or even the flicker of a muscle did she show that she was aware of him in any way.

"Suit yourself," he said finally after a string of expletives. He certainly did have an inventive vocabulary. Must be the business he was in. "You'll eat when you get hungry enough." He went out the door, banging it shut behind him. A short time later, she heard the rhythmic thump of an ax being wielded against wood. It continued for a very long time.

Sabrina got up finally, left the tray where it was and decided to explore the cabin. It was small but artfully arranged, with built-in shelves and drawers that held everything from what looked like a year's supply of food to books, puzzles, even art materials. She also found fishing rods, one entire closet filled just with winter gear including snowshoes and a locked cabinet she suspected contained firearms.

There was no electricity, but the lack didn't bother her much. Perhaps because she'd known so much cosseting over the years, the idea of doing without some of the basic comforts of civilization appealed to her.

There was a pump beside the kitchen sink and another in the bathroom that she'd already used, remembering from something she'd read that she had to prime them first. The bath facilities were especially interesting since there was actually an indoor commode that seemed to operate on a suction principle. She thought it was rather ingenious and certainly beat tromping to the outhouse.

Having an actual bath was another matter, since water would have to be heated on the stove. Or better yet, the fireplace. Confirming what she thought she'd noticed, she checked and found an iron bracket with a hook that could be swung over the fire. Nearby was a large metal kettle complete with sturdy handle. All in all, it looked like a perfectly adequate arrangement. She decided to make use of it before much longer.

She also decided that it was time to eat. Not that

she'd ever intended not to, she just wouldn't give Mac the satisfaction of eating when he said. As much as she possibly could, she intended to thwart him at every turn and get through however long she had to on her own terms.

In the midst of studying the supplies in the pantry, trying to decide between a dried onion soup she thought might not be too bad and canned tuna, her nose twitched. A delectable aroma floated through the open cabin windows—wood smoke and something else, tangy but sweet, tantalizing... Her stomach rumbled.

With utmost reluctance, already suspecting what she would see, Sabrina peered out a back window. Sure enough, there was Mac, stripped to the waist, his burnished chest gleaming in the sun, balanced on his haunches beside a wood fire with a skillet in his hand. A skillet full of freshly caught fish.

No fair. Absolutely no way, no fair. If he thought she could be lured out with a little wild brook trout sautéed with what smelled like almonds and maybe some dried dill thrown in, he was—

Just where had he learned to cook like that? He'd never given her any reason to think he could do more than order takeout.

"It won't work!"

He laughed, his teeth gleaming whitely. "Suit yourself, but you know what they say, nothing in the world tastes as good as freshly caught fish cooked over a wood fire as far from civilization as you can get."

As though to emphasize the wisdom of this observation, he used his fingers to separate a morsel of the delicate fish and popped it into his mouth. His smile was blatantly sensual. "Mmm, best I've ever caught. Don't have any. That will leave more for me." He took another bite, savoring it.

Her stomach rumbled again, loudly. It seemed to have joined the conversation.

"How many did you catch?"

"Six."

"You can't eat all that."

"Sure I can. I may go back for more." He paused and threw in the clincher. "I think I'll have salmon for dinner. There are plenty of them, too. Maybe I'll catch it early, smoke it a little over the fire. That would probably go good with those wild blackberries I saw."

That did it. Here she'd been planning to torture him and he was doing it to her instead. Sabrina came out of the cabin, walked over to the fire and slowly sat down. She never took her eyes off him, unsure what he might do.

What he did was feed her. She tried, belatedly, to go back in for plates and forks, but he wouldn't let her. He insisted the fish was too hot for her fingers. Instead, he plucked morsels from the pan, let them cool slightly and fed them to her by hand.

The succulent food combined with the strangely sensual effect of eating from his hand undid her. She ate, slowly and with unmasked enjoyment, until she couldn't eat another bite.

But right at the end, she got a little of her own back. Before he realized what she intended, she took hold of his wrist. Her eyes on his, she slowly and methodically licked each of the fingers he'd used to feed her. By the time she was finished, his eyes were narrowed to silver shards and she could see the ragged surge of his breath.

"Thanks," she said, standing up suddenly. "I enjoyed that." She resisted the temptation to see how he reacted and went back into the cabin.

Despite her show of bravado, the afternoon dragged. Mac left her strictly alone. She tried to read but without much success. Twice she heard him on the cell phone, but he was speaking too softly for her to make out the words. For an hour or so, he disappeared but she wasn't worried. She knew he would be back.

He returned with the promised salmon and they did have it for dinner, but Mac didn't speak to her during the meal nor did he feed her again. When they'd finished eating and he'd cleared away the dishes, he said, "Rourk has broken off his attack against Century, but he hasn't given me the assurances I want. Not yet." He took the phone out of his pocket and slid it across the table toward her. "Call him. Tell him you want this to end." When she didn't move, he added, "I can have a chopper here an hour after first light. You can be back in New York in time for brunch."

Sabrina stared at the phone. Her eyes lifted to his. Quietly but with perfect diction, she said, "Go to hell."

Chapter 14

Sabrina slept in the bed that night. Mac used the couch. When they awoke the next morning, nothing had changed. He offered her the phone once again. Once again, she refused. He spent the day chopping wood and fishing. This time she cooked, but they ate without speaking.

The cold war—as she quickly came to think of it—continued into the next day and the next. She knew he made and received a few calls, but he said nothing more to her about what was happening with Century. She guessed the most immediate crisis had passed but that her father had yet to give the required assurances.

That didn't surprise her, but it did hurt. A man who would use her as Rourk had done wasn't going to make such major concessions just for her sake. As the hours dragged by, there were times when she was tempted to call him, not to ask for his help but to demand to know how he could have done what he did. There was no point, though. She already knew what he would say—that business was business, there was nothing personal about it, he'd just done what was smart.

He had always compartmentalized his life like that, shutting her away in one corner of it. Mac had seemed inclined to do the same, but he'd changed that night he came back to the apartment, when he'd confided his plans to her. So, too, she had to acknowledge that although he certainly had her shut away at the moment, he'd shut himself away with her.

In fact, if they weren't sleeping apart and not speaking to each other, they could be having a great time.

There were also times when she was tempted to try to do something about that. It hadn't escaped her notice that Mac watched her when he thought she wasn't looking. She saw the flare of desire in his eyes and felt the answering response in herself. It probably wouldn't take very much effort to make them both forget they were estranged.

As another day passed, Sabrina found herself thinking about that more and more. She watched Mac far more than she wanted to, drawn by the rippling play of muscle beneath his skin as he chopped wood or cut back brush from around the cabin. She remembered thinking when she first saw him that his wasn't a body that could come solely from a gym. It reflected a lifetime of hard, manual work toward some worthy purpose.

That evening, when he came into the cabin, she had hot water ready for his bath. On previous evenings, he'd done for himself. Realizing that this time he didn't have to, he looked at her quizzically.

"I made extra," she said. They were the first words she'd spoken to him in days and they made him smile, however unwillingly.

"That's supposed to be about food."

She was so relieved to hear his voice that she smiled in turn. "I did that, too. I hope you're hungry."

He was and she felt a glow of pleasure as he ate the meal she'd prepared. His enjoyment didn't get in the way of their having an actual conversation, although only about strictly neutral topics. Neither one of them mentioned their situation.

Sabrina went to bed that night feeling more hopeful than she had in days. Maybe if she was just patient, he would come to see that what he believed about her was ridiculous. They just needed time.

The next morning, time was very much on her mind once again. She woke to nausea and only just made it into the bathroom before emptying her stomach. Her first thought when she'd recovered enough to think at all was that there must have been something wrong with the previous night's dinner. But she had none of the other symptoms of food poisoning. She wasn't feverish or aching, there were no cold chills, and once her stomach emptied, she rapidly felt better.

She was in the midst of brushing her teeth when she caught sight of herself in the mirror. Her eyes narrowed. Time. She'd always been extremely regular in her cycles. Until now. She was two weeks overdue.

Big deal. She'd been through an awful lot. It was bound to throw her off.

She'd just thrown up.

All right...but that didn't mean she was—

Yes, she was.

There was no way for her to really know and yet she did. Some indefinable sense deep within her signaled the vast, soaring change that had already occurred. Her pulse quickened. Instinctively, her hands went to her flat stomach. Mac's child and hers. She thought back suddenly to what he'd said when he convinced her to marry him so quickly, that she'd made him so wild they'd made love without protection, that she could be pregnant.

She'd believed he was really stretching things just to get her agreement and suspected he thought so, too. Now she had to wonder how he would feel to find out he'd been right.

Her first thought was to tell him immediately, but the inclination vanished almost before it fully formed. The terrible untruth he believed about her was bad enough when it only concerned the two of them. Now there was a third person involved—a helpless, innocent baby. A fierce wave of protectiveness went through her, so intense that it left her shaken.

What kind of mother was she going to be? Strong and brave, putting her child first? Or weak, clinging, caught between a battling father and a husband, nei-

ther of whom seemed to really know who she was or
particularly care.

Ever since Mac had confronted her with his accu-
sations, she'd shied away from thinking about what
they really meant. Now she forced herself to confront
them head-on.

The man she loved with such tender passion had
never indicated that he felt the same way about her.
On the contrary, he had such a low opinion of her that
he believed her capable of essentially prostituting herself to add yet more wealth and power to her father's
empire.

And this was the man she imagined she might
somehow be able to make care for her? He'd already
said he intended to end their marriage. She'd hidden
from the truth long enough. Whatever she did or didn't
do, whatever Rourk conceded or didn't concede, she
couldn't stay with a man who felt that way about her.
Especially not now that she knew there was a child to
protect.

In time, he would have to know about the baby. It
was likely he would want some sort of visitation and
she wouldn't oppose that. A child had a right to know
both its parents. But she would never subject her child
to living in a home where there was no mutual love
and respect.

Her mind made up, she felt strangely calm. She
went into the kitchen and ate a few crackers washed
down by springwater. She would need to see a doctor,
and get on a regular program of supplements. Exercise
would be a good idea, too, but she wouldn't overdo

it. She would take very good care of herself. She
didn't need anyone to do that for her. She would be
fine.

There was silence outside the cabin. Mac wasn't
adding to what was surely a year's supply of firewood.
He was nowhere in sight. She checked the closet and
saw that a fishing rod was missing. In the last couple
of days, he'd taken to being away almost all the wak-
ing hours. She'd resented it terribly, but now it suited
her purposes only too well.

*I can have a chopper here an hour after first light.
You can be back in New York in time for brunch.*

When he'd spoken those words to her a few nights
before, Sabrina hadn't paid much attention to them.
She'd known that she had absolutely no intention of
doing what he wanted. But now they carried an entirely different meaning.

The truck wasn't the only way out. There was another, but it would take some time to organize.

Mac hadn't gotten careless. He always took the cell
phone with him and undoubtedly did the same with
the truck keys. Sabrina spent only a few minutes looking for them on the chance she might get lucky. It
didn't particularly bother her when she didn't.

Taking one of the backpacks from the closet, she
put in several bottles of water, some food, a first-aid
kit and a rain poncho. She left everything else.

In front of the cabin, she paused for a moment to
look back. Her throat tightened and she felt perilously
close to tears, but her resolve held firm. She was doing

the only thing she could. Determinedly, she set off down the trail.

Mac came back sooner than he'd intended. He hadn't meant to, but thoughts of how it had been between them at dinner drew him irresistibly. Try though he did, he couldn't reconcile the woman who heated bathwater for him and made him laugh about the foibles of temperamental chefs, with a scheming seductress driven solely by greed.

It bothered him that he'd never given Sabrina a chance to tell him her version of things. He was a fair man by nature and even though he was convinced of what had happened, he still could at least have listened to her. As far-fetched as it seemed, maybe there was some sort of mitigating circumstance. The mere thought of that struck him as pathetic and he threw it off with disgust. But he still found himself walking back into the clearing hours sooner than he'd planned.

When he didn't find Sabrina outside in the warm sunshine, he assumed she was within. His surprise upon stepping into the cabin to utter silence cut right through him. Quickly, he checked the bedroom and bath. Both were empty. She was nowhere to be found.

Deliberately, he took several deep breaths and forced himself to think clearly. It was a beautiful day. She'd gotten bored with her own company and gone for a walk. Undoubtedly, she was well within the sound of his voice.

"Sabrina!" Standing outside the cabin, he called her name. There was no response. He tried again. "Sabrina!'' Only a jackdaw answered, his hooting *coo* sounding like mockery.

Silence returned to the pine forest, bringing with it the realization of the small details he'd scarcely noticed during his hasty search of the cabin. A closet door left partly ajar, an empty box of crackers on the kitchen counter. He ran back in, checking much more thoroughly and soon knew the truth. One of the packs was gone along with some rain gear. Several water bottles were missing.

The idiot. The beautiful, maddening idiot.

Mac started down the trail at a run. He reached the clearing fully expecting to see the truck still there. Why not, when the keys to it were in his pocket? But there was nothing except a few tire tracks in the soft dirt and a haunting feeling of emptiness. A flutter of white caught his eye. A note was set on a nearby boulder, held in place by a small rock.

I'll make sure the truck gets returned.

Sabrina

P.S. Anyone who can rewire an electrical stove can hot-wire an engine.

Mac was still cursing an hour later when he trudged back into the cabin and called for the chopper.

Chapter 15

"What do you mean, where is she?" Rourk demanded. His hands balled into fists, his face flushed, he stared at Mac incredulously. "You were the one who had her. How the hell could you not know where she is?"

More worried than angry, but furious all the same, Mac growled. "Cut the bull. I know perfectly well she must be here. I just want to make sure she's all right."

Glaring at the other man, he added, "You win, okay? You can stage as many raids against Century as you damn well like. You and I can spend all our time fighting each other and maybe destroy both our companies in the process. I don't care anymore. I just want to know where Sabrina is!"

Even as he said the words he knew they were true. He didn't care what she'd done or why. It no longer mattered. All he wanted was to have her back, to have another chance.

The thought of her making her way down the mountain alone had haunted him ever since he realized she was gone. He'd waited through an agonizing few hours until the chopper could reach him, then insisted the pilot fly along all the major highways leading south on the chance that the truck might be spotted. It wasn't, but Mac hadn't been willing to concede defeat until there was only enough fuel left to get him to New York. Once there, he'd gone directly to Rourk's office, brushing past the secretaries and even a security guard who tried to stop him. Face-to-face with Rourk, he demanded the truth.

"I'm telling you," the older man shouted, "I don't know where she is! But, by God, if she's come to any harm—" He started toward Mac only to stop when he saw the look on his son-in-law's face. More quietly, he said, "You mean that?"

"Mean what?" All Mac could focus on was the chance that Rourk really didn't know where Sabrina was. That would mean she was still out there somewhere, maybe stuck, possibly hurt. His stomach knotted.

"That you don't care about the business end, just about Sabrina."

"I said I wanted to know where she was. I care about that."

Rourk stared at him for a long moment. The eyes, so similar to Sabrina's yet so different, seemed to penetrate right through him. Abruptly, Rourk threw back his head and laughed. "God, I remember what it was like to fool myself that way. Tell myself I didn't have to feel, that I could just pick which parts of life I wanted to deal with and leave the rest."

He stepped closer, his expression suddenly bleak. "You know what, *that's* bull. I spent years after Sabrina's mother died building a wall around myself. I didn't even let my own daughter get through it. I got to the point that when I saw one last chance to take something I wanted, I grabbed it with no thought to what it would mean to her."

A sickening hollowness opened up on Mac. He stared at Rourk in dawning horror. "What are you talking about?"

"You know damn well. I'm talking about this last run I made on Century. And it is the *last* run. I never expected you to play so tough or so dirty. Frankly, if I'd known you had this in you, I wouldn't have been in any hurry to see you and Sabrina married."

He took another hard look at Mac and relented slightly. "Well, maybe not. Maybe I still would have wanted it since *she* did so much. Anyway, I figured in the long run we'd all be better off if the two companies merged, but I didn't want to just go to you with that. You'd rejected it too many times already. I decided to make one more try, see if I couldn't gain enough leverage to make you decide for yourself that a merger was the way to go."

"But Sabrina helped you. She told you how I planned to stop you."

"Like hell she did. Sabrina didn't tell me anything. She's the most loyal person imaginable." Sadly but with stark honesty, Rourk said, "Her loyalty is to you. All things considered, that's the way it should be."

"No," Mac murmured. He felt as though he was choking. He tried to breathe but it hurt so much, it didn't seem worth bothering. "No, it isn't."

"Sit down," Rourk said. Without waiting, he pushed him into the chair next to the desk. "Jeez, you look like hell." A grin split his face. "You're really in love with her, aren't you?"

Mac nodded dumbly as the full realization of what he'd tried so hard to deny to himself washed over him. What was the point of trying to deny it any longer? He was beaten, finished, done. The woman who had loved him, and whom he loved, however stupid he'd been about realizing it, was gone. And he had no idea where. He had to think, figure something out, plan...but nothing was happening. All he could do was hurt.

"Detectives," he muttered. "I need detectives, the best...they'll know how to find her." They had to. He wouldn't be able to live if they didn't.

Rourk looked at him for a long moment. He put a hand on Mac's shoulder and said gently, "Naaah, you don't need that. You need some food." When Mac looked up, startled, he added, "*Italian* food."

Pavarotti was belting one out over the restaurant sound system. A couple of waiters were seated at a table in the front, playing cards. Lunch was finished and it was hours yet to the dinner trade. Time for everyone to catch a breather.

Sylvia was seated on a stool beside the bar. Sabrina

was next to her. She'd arrived just a short time before. Nearby, Jenny played on the floor, scooping up jacks. Sabrina looked at her and let out a long sigh.

Sylvia shot her a quick glance, one of many she'd been giving her ever since a white-faced and hollow-eyed Sabrina walked in the door. Sylvia had taken one look at her and shooed Joseph away, knowing he would explode before she got more than a word out of her mouth.

"Let me get this straight," Sylvia said. "You want to work full-time?"

"For a while," Sabrina amended. She'd thought about it very carefully on the way home, first in the truck, then on the airplane. She was sure she'd hit on the right solution. "I want to get a restaurant up and running. It'll be a tremendous amount of work, I know, but it's what I need. In six months or so, I should have it set. After that, I'll need to taper off a little, work a part-time schedule. I'd like you and Joseph to come in as partners. I know you've been interested in expanding, and this would be a good way to do it."

Sylvia nodded thoughtfully. "It makes sense. We've been hoping you'd feel this way. But what does Mac think?"

Sabrina took a sip of her mineral water. "He's not involved in this."

"You can bet he's going to have an opinion about it all the same. Husbands are like that."

Sabrina's lips compressed. She looked away quickly. "I don't think he's going to be my husband much longer. He really doesn't want to be."

Sylvia's mouth dropped open. She started to speak but broke off, distracted by two events that occurred simultaneously. One was that a hovering Joseph suddenly started toward the front door with murder in his eyes. The other was that the door—locked while the restaurant was closed—was quivering inward, the glass set in it trembling under a rain of blows.

"Open up!"

"Oh my God!" Sabrina's hand went to her mouth. She stared in disbelief as Joseph flung the door open one step ahead of Mac's pounding it down.

"Whaddya you think you're doing coming in here like this?" Joseph demanded. He gestured toward Sabrina. "And what's she doing here? How come the two of you aren't still on your honeymoon and how come she's looking the way she does?" His lip curled in disgust. "I thought you were a man, the kind who could take care of a woman right, but instead—"

"That's enough," Mac said. He brushed past Joseph and walked straight toward Sabrina. The two waiters, both young men of the large persuasion, started to rise but Joseph waved them back. "You don't have to talk to him if you don't want," he called to Sabrina.

Just as well since she didn't think she could talk. Sylvia, however, had no such problem. She slipped off the stool, planted herself firmly in front of Sabrina and said, "Now look here. I don't know what you think you're doing, but you can't treat Sabrina like this. She's my friend and I won't let you—"

"Here," Mac said, picking Sylvia off the floor and handing her to her husband. "Take care of this."

He turned back to give his full attention to his own wife. She, too, had stood and was looking at him shakily. But her chin was up. He was glad to see that. He couldn't stand the idea of her being afraid of him. That would be even worse than her not caring at all.

Pavarotti was going into the big windup. Violins were playing in the background. Joseph, Sylvia and the waiters were watching. Several more people had come out of the kitchen to see what was going on.

Mac didn't hesitate. Right there in front of everyone, he went down on one knee, took Sabrina's hand in his and said, "Sabrina Giacanna Talveston, will you be my wife?"

Joseph snorted. "He forgot they're married?" He didn't get any further when Sylvia elbowed him in the ribs.

Mac's voice thickened. "I know I'm asking a tremendous amount, but can you forgive me, please? If you can't, I'll understand, but I love you with all my heart. If I can spend the rest of my life making you happy, I'll savor every moment." Softly, so softly, he added, "Please, Sabrina, please abide with me."

Tears slipped down Sabrina's cheeks. She didn't care. She was too busy sinking to her own knees beside Mac, cupping his beloved face in her hands, looking deeply into the eyes filled with emotion that mirrored her own. On a note of wonder, she whispered, "Oh, yes, Mac. Oh, yes, please."

Epilogue

"I love it when you ask so nicely," Mac said. He turned over on his side and grinned at his wife. They were lying beside the pool of the Jersey house. The day was warm, the sky cloudless, the hilltop silent save for the drone of industrious bees in the hibiscus. The servants were once more discreetly absent. He had just devoted the last several hours to demonstrating how he felt about her, and was well satisfied with the results.

So, by all appearances, was Sabrina. Her eyes were wide and languorous, her mouth slightly swollen. Save for a necklace of pink-hued pearls draped between her breasts and the rings on her left hand, she was gloriously, delightfully bare. The thought flitted through his mind that she really was turning the same color as the apricots she liked so much, and every bit as succulent.

"As I recall," she murmured, "I was digging my nails into your back at the time."

He shrugged. "A small price to pay." So swept up had he been in his own pleasure that he hadn't felt her scratches. But then he knew they couldn't be very bad. Sabrina would never hurt him. Just as he would never again hurt her.

Gently, he brushed the back of his bronzed fingers across her cheek. She smiled and turned her head slightly, enough to touch her lips softly to his hand. The caress, fleeting as it was, sent a bolt of pleasure through him that made him smile wryly. After the excesses of the last few hours, he should have been far beyond arousal. But where his beautiful, seductive wife was concerned, that never seemed to be the case.

With a laugh that sounded more like a growl, he rolled over and let himself drop into the pool. Sabrina sat up in surprise, watching him, and laughed. He surfaced, shaking the water from his ebony hair so that a spray of diamond droplets struck her heated skin. She yelped and tried to reach for a towel, but he grabbed it, tugging hard. Sabrina wouldn't let go, he wouldn't stop. Both of them were grinning as he drew her toward him until she was just teetering on the edge of the pool.

"I don't want to get wet again," she murmured even as her eyes swept over the broad, burnished expanse of his shoulders. "I'm all nice and comfy."

His brows arched. "Comfy? That's what you call what I made you feel? Comfy?"

Before his male ire could rise any further, she

grinned. ''You know, maybe I wouldn't mind getting wet after all.'' Gracefully, hardly rippling the water, she slid into the pool and wound her arms around her husband's neck. He stretched out on his back, his powerful arms and legs keeping them afloat. For a time, they were content to merely drift, but soon enough the closeness of their bodies and the ever-present heat of desire had their inevitable effects.

''Are you sure we won't drown?'' Sabrina asked playfully as he drew her into the shallower end of the pool, his intent clear in the smoldering glance he gave her. His answer was a kiss that robbed her of breath and left her clinging to him.

She gasped when his mouth grazed first one nipple, then the other, his tongue laving her with long, firm strokes. Helplessly, she moved against him, her hands stroking the powerful lines of his back and buttocks, urging him closer. He complied, slipping his hands beneath her thighs to part and lift her legs, then winding them around his hips. As the warm, crystalline water lapped at them, he entered her slowly, drawing out the moment of his complete possession until she was writhing with demand.

When he joined them fully at last, Sabrina cried out softly, welcoming him into her body with a generosity and passion that never failed to touch a chord deep within him. Although he thought to draw out their pleasure, he found that he could not. Their hunger for each other was simply too great. They crested swiftly in a long, drawn out burst of pleasure that seemed to go on forever before leaving them at last replete and exhausted.

With what he assumed was the last of his strength—although where Sabrina was concerned, that was never a safe assumption—Mac lifted his drowsily content wife from the water and laid her beside the pool, then swiftly joined her. He stretched out and drew her close. They rested for some time, but neither felt any urge to sleep. Sabrina rose after a while and poured two glasses of fruit juice. Returning to kneel beside Mac, she offered him one. ''To the future,'' she said with a smile.

''The future,'' he agreed. They touched glasses and drank.

''Are you still serious about the restaurant?'' he asked.

Sabrina nodded. She reached over to the bowl on a nearby table and helped herself to an apricot. Biting into it, she said, ''I think it's right for me. The startup phase will be pretty intensive, but then you'll be busy, too.''

Mac grimaced. He was still getting used to his decision to merge Century with Talveston. Barely had he broken that news to his father and brothers—who had actually taken it fairly well—when Rourk stunned them all by announcing that he would be retiring soon. He would stay on long enough to help Mac get everything up and running, but after that he had plans of his own. He wanted to travel, maybe write, do some of the things he'd put off all these years.

''Not too busy,'' Mac said. He stroked a hand up

her arm and lightly cupped her breast. Dimly, in the back of his mind, he thought her breasts were fuller of late, even more exquisitely beautiful.

"You know," he said as he drew her closer, "there's only one thing that would make this even more perfect."

"What's that?"

"I know we haven't talked about it, but I really like kids." He looked into her eyes. "I don't want to pressure you or anything. There's no rush. It's just that I wouldn't want to wait *too* long."

Sabrina's smile deepened. "But we seem to do things in a rush and it works out fine."

His eyes gleamed. The thought of her swelling with their child was a sudden, piercing delight. "You mean you'd be willing…soon…?"

Her smile spread, lighting her eyes, reaching right into him with love and tenderness. And the promise to fill a lifetime.

"I have something to tell you," she said.

And did.

* * * * *

SILHOUETTE

Sensation

COMING NEXT MONTH

DISCOVERED: DADDY Marilyn Pappano

Daddy Knows Last

No one knew who'd fathered Faith Harper's baby and she was refusing to name the culprit. Nine months later, agent Nick Russo unexpectedly returned to town and Faith couldn't believe he had forgotten their earth-shattering night together. Now what was she going to do?

ANGUS'S LOST LADY Marie Ferrarella

Private detective Angus MacDougall was used to finding missing persons. But the woman standing before him was a different prospect. *She* had absolutely no idea who she was! And no clue as to why someone had taken a shot at her...

AN HONOURABLE MAN Margaret Watson

Two years ago grief had made Luke McKinley go too far; one wrong move had cost him his career as a cop. He still felt a burning anger at the woman he blamed for his dismissal so he was amazed at her nerve, coming to him now and asking for his help. Why would he put his life on the line for her?

WALKING AFTER MIDNIGHT Alicia Scott

Heartbreakers

Sabrina Duncan lived in the shadows of the city and was unfortunate enough to see a serial killer meet his most recent victim. That made Police Lieutenant Thomas Lain her protector. But despite their mutual attraction, Sabrina's past lay between them...

COMING NEXT MONTH FROM

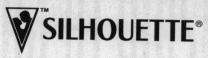 SILHOUETTE®

Intrigue
Danger, deception and desire

THE VALENTINE HOSTAGE Dawn Stewardson
RANSOM MY HEART Gayle Wilson
THROUGH THE EYES OF A CHILD Laura Kenner
RUNAWAY HEART Saranne Dawson

Special Edition
Satisfying romances packed with emotion

VALENTINE BABY Gina Wilkins
UNEXPECTED MUMMY Sherryl Woods
FOR THE LOVE OF SAM Jackie Merritt
THE PATERNITY QUESTION Andrea Edwards
THE COUGAR Lindsay McKenna
MISSION: MOTHERHOOD Jule McBride

Desire
Provocative, sensual love stories for the woman of today

THE COWBOY CRASHES A WEDDING Anne McAllister
CHAMPAGNE GIRL Diana Palmer
THE HARD-TO-TAME TEXAN Lass Small
BRIDE CANDIDATE NO. 9 Susan Crosby
LAST OF THE JOEVILLE LOVERS Anne Eames
COURTSHIP IN GRANITE RIDGE Barbara McCauley

ELIZABETH GAGE

When Dusty brings home her young fiancé, he
is everything her mother Rebecca Lowell could
wish for her daughter, *and for herself...*

The Lowell family's descent into darkness
begins with one bold act, one sin
committed in an otherwise blameless life.
This time there's no absolution in...

Confession

MIRA

AVAILABLE FROM JANUARY 1999

2 FREE

books and a surprise gift!

We would like to take this opportunity to thank you for reading this Silhouette® book by offering you the chance to take TWO more specially selected titles from the Sensation™ series absolutely FREE! We're also making this offer to introduce you to the benefits of the Reader Service™—

- ★ FREE home delivery
- ★ FREE gifts and competitions
- ★ FREE monthly newsletter
- ★ Books available before they're in the shops
- ★ Exclusive Reader Service discounts

Accepting these FREE books and gift places you under no obligation to buy; you may cancel at any time, even after receiving your free shipment. Simply complete your details and return the entire page to the address below. *You don't even need a stamp!*

✂

YES! Please send me 2 free Sensation books and a surprise gift. I understand that unless you hear from me, I will receive 4 superb new titles every month for just £2.70 each, postage and packing free. I am under no obligation to purchase any books and may cancel my subscription at any time. The free books and gift will be mine to keep in any case.

S9EA

Ms/Mrs/Miss/Mr.................................Initials ....
BLOCK CAPITALS PLEASE

Surname ....

Address ....

....

....Postcode...............................

Send this whole page to:
THE READER SERVICE, FREEPOST CN81, CROYDON, CR9 3WZ
(Eire readers please send coupon to: P.O. BOX 4546, DUBLIN 24.)

Offer not valid to current Reader Service subscribers to this series. We reserve the right to refuse an application and applicants must be aged 18 years or over. Only one application per household. Terms and prices subject to change without notice. Offer expires 31st July 1999. As a result of this application you may receive further offers from Harlequin Mills & Boon and other carefully selected companies. If you would prefer not to share in this opportunity please write to The Data Manager at the address above.

Silhouette Sensation is a registered trademark used under license.

He's a cop, she's his prime suspect

MARY LYNN BAXTER

HARD CANDY

He's crossed the line no cop ever should.
He's involved with a suspect—his
prime suspect.

Falling for the wrong man is far down her
list of troubles.

Until he arrests her for murder.

Available from 18th December 1998